KODIAK

DELTA JAMES

Copyright © 2020 by Delta James

Published by Stormy Night Publications and Design, LLC.
www.StormyNightPublications.com

Cover design by Korey Mae Johnson
www.koreymaejohnson.com

Images by Shutterstock/Body Stock, DepositPhoto/PiLens, DepositPhotos/Svetas, DepositPhotos/nejron, and DepositPhotos/Lukasok

All rights reserved.

1st Print Edition. November 2020

ISBN-13: 9798573970011

FOR AUDIENCES 18+ ONLY

This book is intended for adults only. Spanking and other sexual activities represented in this book are fantasies only, intended for adults.

CHAPTER ONE

Two years previously

Alex Kingston hated his life at the moment. Two weeks ago, he'd drawn the short straw and had been forced to be the representative of their park ranger unit at the mandatory annual conference in Seattle.

"I swear I'll pay anybody a thousand dollars to go instead of me," he'd offered.

His fellow rangers had all laughed; Alex hadn't been amused.

"Seriously, King, it won't be that bad," one of the others had offered. "You could have fun."

"I'd rather have a root canal," Alex had growled. "Two thousand."

"No way, you dodged the bullet last time. It's your turn."

"Shit," he snarled. "I hope a group of hippy protestors come up and stage a sit-in and the lot of you have to freeze your butts off babysitting them."

He'd stalked out of the park ranger station, gone home, packed, and was now walking the rain-drenched sidewalks of Seattle. He hated the lower forty-eight in general, but it was mating season on Shuyak. The need to find a willing female to breed had only been inflamed by the allure of the beautiful women of the city who favored fashion over practicality. The conference had concluded today. He had separated off from the other rangers in order to take care of his need. Although he knew he wouldn't find one of his kind to rut with, mounting a woman from behind and fucking her aggressively would at least assuage the profound instinct that was threatening to overwhelm him.

He could hear the loud and lively Irish band playing music as it blared out onto the city streets each time the door opened. He entered the pub and allowed his eyes to adjust to the muted darkness. Listening to the band playing, he recognized several songs from his twin brother's collection of CDs.

King headed over to the bar and positioned himself where he could see both the band and the rest of the pub easily. The two bartenders were busy, efficient, and friendly. They were close by, mixing drinks and drawing drafts when a tall, curvaceous, mahogany-haired beauty walked in. She was wearing rust-colored riding breeches tucked into high, black riding boots with a billowy white silk shirt that hung loosely past her ass.

"Here comes trouble," one of the bartenders said, chuckling lustily.

"Yeah, I wouldn't mind getting a taste of that," responded the other.

King smiled as he felt his dormant cock come to life and throb. If things went as he planned, the bartender would have to wait his turn; Trouble would be occupied for the night. If she didn't live close by, he had spotted several spots in the alley and in the adjacent park that could suffice for what he had in mind… at least to start. After things had quieted down in the hotel, he could smuggle her in and use her hard until morning, before calling her a cab and returning home to Alaska. She sidled up to the bar, her ass grazing the front of his jeans.

"What'll it be, Flynn?" asked the bartender who was

going to be disappointed.

So, Trouble had a name. Flynn. Interesting that this woman—whose figure so screamed breedable female that even a loose-fitting shirt couldn't hide it—had a strong, masculine name.

Smiling, she replied, "The usual."

The man smiled and produced a bottle from underneath the bar—McCallan's fifty-year-old single malt. The woman had expensive tastes. No matter, he had no intention of courting her with flowers or anything else. He watched as she took a long, slow sip of the liquor, giving the slightest shiver as it invaded and warmed her body. He sniffed the air discreetly and picked up the slightest whiff of her arousal. He had no doubt Flynn had come searching for someone to have sex with. Fortunately for her, he was more than willing and able to accommodate her.

King straightened to his full height, peering over her shoulder, and treating himself to a good look down the front of her shirt. His eyes grazed her body. She had long, powerful legs and a well-defined feminine figure—large breasts, a small waist, and hips that could accommodate a man between them. The silk shirt wafting just past her bottom cupped it almost like a lover's caress. Had she been his woman, the way she was dressed to visit a bar on her own would have provoked not a loving touch, but a harsh spanking, followed by a rough fucking. King's cock continued to throb while his hand itched to spank her hard.

He inhaled more deeply. Her scent was an intoxicating mixture of the perfume she wore, combined with the slightest whiff of horses, fresh hay, and good leather. He erased what little distance was left between them as they lounged against the bar railing in the crowded room. He pressed the front of his jeans against her backside, allowing her to feel his need. Whether by instinct or design, Flynn settled back against him. Glancing back over her shoulder, she smiled, seeming to like what she saw.

They stood without speaking, enjoying the music and

their whiskey. King switched his drink to the hand that was furthest from the bar, placing the other on her hip where it would be next to impossible to see. She made no move to dislodge his hand or indicate its presence wasn't welcome, saying nothing and not moving away. His hand slipped down to the back of her leg and returned to cup her ass as the rhythmic music played on. She snuggled back into him, shivering again, and giving a small sigh of pleasure. Slipping his hand around the front of her hip, he cupped her mons before dipping his hand between her legs and securing her body against his. Her head dropped back to rest against his muscular chest, allowing his hard staff to separate her butt cheeks even through their clothes. She slid her hand down to cover his.

From his greater height, King had an even better look down the front of her shirt, allowing him to see the swell of her breasts as they peeked out of what appeared to be a lilac lace corset. King's erection continued to harden as he imaged all that the corset didn't reveal, and the pleasure he would take in unlacing it, but not before he'd spanked the luxurious bottom that was pressed firmly against him and spread her legs to sink his length into her pussy.

Flynn said nothing but continued to sip her scotch slowly.

King slid his hand from where it had been resting at the apex of her legs up under her shirt, stopping at the waistband of her breeches. The band played on with the audience clapping and singing enthusiastically. When she didn't move away, he unfastened the snap and lowered the zipper, slipping his hand inside and running it back down through the silky curls he found there. Flynn stifled a moan but parted her thighs, giving him greater access.

His finger found the swollen nub that lay just beyond, and he stroked it gently. Her reply to the unasked question was to rub against him sensually. Grinning, King's caress grew bolder as his fingers parted her lower lips and delved for the entrance to her core. The feel of her buttocks nestled against his engorged member was the most exquisite torture. One finger and then a second, penetrated her wet heat. He leaned forward and growled low in her ear. She moaned and leaned harder against him. Out of the corner of his eye, he saw the two bartenders and knew they were well aware of his actions.

Flynn's breath quickened; the diamond shards of her nipples pressed against the corset and his arm that was wrapped over her shoulder. She chewed on her lip to try and silence the small whimpers that threatened to escape as her body raced towards an impending climax. Her pussy pulsed around his fingers and her muscles stiffened in anticipation. King plunged his fingers into her more rapidly and watched as she reached the apex of the climb to full release and then withdrew, not allowing her to achieve it.

Bringing his hand back into view he licked his fingers as her eyes widened and nostrils flared in both arousal and frustration. She tried to move away from him, but he caught her about the waist and pulled her back into the cradle of his pelvis, ensuring she could feel his need. When she tried to reach under her shirt to close the opening of her breeches, he growled again, but this time in warning and not desire.

"What I unfasten stays that way until I tell you otherwise," he whispered in her ear.

"Says who?" she mocked him, trying to move away.

This time instead of locking her against him by the waist, he dropped his arm over her shoulder so that it lay between the valley of her breasts and once again cupped her mons possessively. The scent of her assailed him and the pounding of his cock intensified. Turning her around to face him, his head descended, his lips locking with hers in a kiss that promised both passion and strength.

Tossing a fifty-dollar bill on the bar, he asked, "Do you have a private office?"

The bartender who had first called her trouble nodded and pointed to an exit to the left of the bar. Wrapping his arm around her, King propelled Flynn out of the cacophony of sound that was the central bar, through the door, down the hall and into the small office that was filled mostly with a large desk. King smiled. It would do nicely.

"Hey, I don't know what you think is going to happen…" she started.

King said nothing, spinning her around and forcing her over the edge of the desk. She was human and as his mate—the thought that she was his mate came unbidden—she would need to learn to submit to him and those lessons started now.

He spun the belief that Flynn was his mate around in his mind, like one would swirl a fine whiskey in a heavy, crystal glass before consuming it, and found the idea intoxicating and comforting at the same time. It seemed that the reason he'd been unable to find his mate before now was that she'd been in Seattle and not at home in Alaska.

He flipped her shirttail up, stripped her breeches down to her knees, exposing her perfect, ivory buttocks. The idea of being able to rut with this female was almost irresistible. The image of watching his cock thrusting in and out as his hips butted her punished backside caused it to become painfully hard. King knew in this position the firm texture of her buttocks would bounce nicely with every swat. Their beautiful pale color would pinken and then deepen to red as he punished her, taught her to yield, and that her place was either beneath him on her back or in front of him on her knees. He longed to suckle her tits, alternately nipping, sucking, and laving his tongue across their turgid peaks.

Before she could speak again, he brought his hand down on her left cheek hard enough for color to bloom and to leave a handprint. King landed another harsh blow to her other cheek, before beginning to rhythmically tattoo her entire backside with enough force that he heard her catch her breath. If she thought she would stoically endure his treatment, she had another thought coming. His kind did not mate quietly or gently, there was always a primal energy that drove it, often bordering on violence. When she tried to get up, he forced her back into place, pinning her down by the neck.

"That's enough," she hissed as he continued to deliver what he was sure was a long overdue spanking.

He made a sound that contained elements of both a growl and a roar. King rained hard slaps down on her buttocks. Flynn squirmed and tried to get away, but he held her fast and continued to punish her now blushing globes. She fought him in earnest, but she was no match for his size, strength, and determination. When she finally acquiesced to his control, chewing on her lower lip to keep from crying out, he ceased his torment and trailed his finger in the cleft of her bottom until he reached her dark rosebud. She struggled again and tried to rise, but he had her trapped. He removed his hand and delivered a series of stinging blows, causing her to yowl.

King placed his hand between her thighs, pinching the sensitive skin when she didn't soften to his touch and open her legs. He scented the air, smiling as the perfume of her increased arousal swirled all around him. He slid his hand between her legs. The feel of her slickened outer lips caused the throbbing of his cock to increase. He meant to fuck her hard and leave her spent, sated, and chastised. Then he would take her home and finish the rut in his bed. He shoved two fingers up into her cunt, plunging them in and out causing her to writhe on the desk.

When he moved from her side to directly behind her and kicked her legs as far apart as they could go, she protested and was rewarded with another hard swat to what he was sure was a very painful bottom. He continued to grasp her neck to hold her in place. He used his other hand to unbutton his jeans, freeing his cock and preparing to mount her from behind. The hand from her neck moved to the top of her shoulder, as he grasped her hip with the other to keep her from moving out of position for his possession. He groaned as he sank to her depth and felt her velvety sheath for the first time. His thrusting was powerful and confident. The pulsing that ran from the tip of his cock to the base was the most sensual anguish he'd ever endured. Her body was ratcheting up to achieve orgasm and he increased his plunging to send her over the edge. Flynn cried out and her body shook with the intensity.

"There's my good mate," he leaned over and whispered as he continued to stroke her heated sheath.

Her body shuddered in acutely aroused response. King increased the rhythm and pace of his thrusting, allowing her little time to recover. Her body came alight in renewed answer to his call, surrendering herself to his need. Her breathing was heavy and ragged as she thrashed beneath him, trying to get away. He held her firmly in place as he continued to pound her pussy. His cock hammered her, scraping her vaginal walls with its roughened texture. He continued his sensual domination until she climaxed again. He gave one last, hard ferocious thrust deep inside her. Flynn screamed in ecstasy, her pussy convulsing and clamping down hard as she writhed in his hold. Her sheath contracted and spasmed rhythmically, greedily milking his cock for every last drop of his seed, savoring every bit of bliss that she could from the encounter.

King withdrew from her, watching his cum dribble out of her as her pussy gaped from his hard use. The rut had him within its thrall and all he wanted was to get her naked and on her back so he could start again. When he fucked her hard enough and long enough to take the edge off, he would take her home and teach her the ways of his clan.

He spanked her swollen labia, pussy, and clit and she cried out.

"I'm going to get a cab. You'll stay here until I come for you and then we'll head to your place." He stroked her very red backside thoughtfully. "Before I'm done, your pussy will be far more sore than your ass. You will learn from the get-go to submit to me." He fingered her bottom hole a second time and she squirmed, causing him to swat each cheek and between her legs again. "I'll take that hole and your mouth in due time, but for now, your cunt will be well used."

He hitched up his jeans, rebuttoned them, and headed into the alley, walking towards the street to hail a taxi.

∙ ∙ ∙ ∙ ∙ ∙ ∙

Flynn lay there, stunned and spent. True, she had come into the bar looking to get laid, but what she had just experienced had not been on her agenda. It had gone far beyond casual sex. Her nipples were still painfully hard, pressing against the confines of her corset. His cum was dripping down the inside of her thigh and she knew her pussy and ass would be feeling the effects of his use for days if not a week or more.

She shook her head, trying to break whatever spell he had woven around her. How the hell had she allowed this to happen? She should have said no when his hand had rested on her hip, swatted his hand away when he'd cupped the juncture of her thighs the first time. She blushed remembering the way she had wantonly rubbed against him as he'd fingered her in the crowded bar and when lust had surged through her system as he'd pinned her down and spanked her before mounting her like a bitch in heat.

And now, he'd gone for a cab with the express intent of taking her back to her place and repeating the whole thing. There might be nothing she could do about what she had allowed to happen, with little more than a token protest, but she could damn well ensure it never happened again. She knew Randy and Lyle, the bartenders, would never give the guy any information about her. She wished he'd gone back through the bar, but he hadn't.

She straightened her clothing, opened the door to the office and quickly exited the bar, pushing and shoving her way through the throng. She found her car and pulled out of the parking lot, spying the man who'd fucked her as he came out the front door and seemed to roar at the moon.

Flynn took a circuitous route home, ensuring she hadn't been followed, until she reached the marina where she kept her houseboat. She didn't realize she'd been holding her breath until she closed and locked the door behind her. Shaking herself, she headed to her cabin to take a shower and crawled into bed.

CHAPTER TWO

Present day

The jarring notes of her phone interrupted her exhausted slumber.

"Flynn Montgomery. If this isn't life or death, fuck off and die," she growled into the phone.

"Jesus, Flynn good to talk to you too," laughed her brother.

Flynn sighed, "Seriously, Ben. You'd better have a monumentally good reason to be waking me up at this hour. I just got back from New Zealand…" she glanced at her phone to see the time, "Arrgghh, three hours ago."

"Good. Then you've had some sleep. Do you know who Henry Koto is?"

"Of Koto Development?"

Koto Development was one of the largest development firms in the world with services that included architectural, engineering, and construction. Having been founded in the Pacific Northwest by Julian Koto, the old man had achieved regional prominence before retiring and leaving the firm to his three sons. Henry was the oldest and had led the firm to global domination in their field with projects in Japan,

Dubai, the UAE, and all across Europe.

"One and the same. He fancies himself something of an artistic photographer. One of the galleries in Pike Place Market is giving him a show…"

"I wonder how much that cost him?" Flynn said with a smile.

"Don't know; don't care. His proposed show is wildlife stills of the mammals unique to the Pacific Northwest. He's already got wolves, otters, and several others. What he wants now are caribou and Kodiaks and he wants Daredevil Adventures to help him get them. He wants to photograph them in their natural environment."

"Does he know how stupid that is? Especially at this time of year? The caribou are bad enough, but Kodiaks? Bad idea."

"He knows and doesn't care. I tried explaining that to him, but he's willing to pay us a lot of money…and I do mean a lot. Like you could pay off your student loans a lot."

"Why don't you take him?" Flynn grumbled.

"Because," he said in a mocking, upper-crust tone, "he wants the youngest professor ever to achieve tenure at U of W to take him."

"Henry Koto knows who I am?"

"Yep. He quoted several of your articles. In particular, he liked the one you did on paleobiology regarding Kodiaks being the possible source of the Sasquatch legends. But you can talk to him when we meet with him."

Flynn sighed. She loved her brother with all of her heart, and his business, Daredevil Adventures, was just starting to take off. He had garnered a reputation for providing exciting, sometimes high-risk, sojourns into remote places to do unconventional things. Ben was an all-around outdoorsman and an ex-SEAL who worked as a guide for anything oceanic. He often tapped Flynn as a guide between her obligations to the university. She had become highly sought after in both roles. Her work in paleobiology and arctic studies allowed her to combine legend, myth, and fact into a fascinating narrative.

"I suppose I could come in tomorrow," she said reluctantly.

"Ah… yeah… well… he wants to meet with us this morning at ten. He's sending his car for you at nine."

"Ben!" she cried in exasperation. "I'm exhausted."

"Did the Stevensons give you a rough time?"

"No, they were great. They always are. But trekking in the wilderness in New Zealand isn't exactly a walk down First Avenue and the flight home was twenty-two and a half hours. I look like something the cat dragged in."

"Use more make-up. Please, Flynn? I'm serious. This is really important to him. Kodiaks are hard to capture on film close up…"

"Because they're territorial and aggressive. There are a lot of cautionary tales about trying."

"Thus, why he wants to do it and to hire us. Who better than a renowned expert on Kodiaks with an unparalleled reputation as a back-country guide? Then you add in a bunch of doctorates behind her name and the notoriety of finding the fossilized baculum of a polar bear and selling it for twenty-five thousand dollars to a private collector?"

"I really do hate you," Flynn grumbled, throwing back the covers and sitting up on the edge of the bed.

"I know, but I'm still your favorite brother…"

"You're my only brother, butthead."

"See you in the car. He's picking me up after you. You have to admit it, a client that sends a limo for you…"

"So, he doesn't have to be bothered fighting Seattle traffic…"

"Flynn, promise me you'll play nice."

"On three hours' sleep? I'm not promising you anything. See you later."

She ended the call, stared at the phone for a moment and shook her head. Even if he wasn't her only brother, she was sure he'd be her favorite. They'd always been close, but when their parents were both killed trying to summit Mount

McKinley, also known as Denali, Ben had left college and become a longshoreman in order to convince the authorities that he could be her guardian. He'd given up his dream of becoming a marine biologist. How could she not support him in making his company a success?

Flynn jumped in the bath and closed her eyes, allowing the rainfall showerhead to beat down on her. She could feel her desire awakening. It had been way too long since she'd found any sexual release—at her own hand, not to mention with a man. As usual when she was alone and tired and stressed, the unbidden memory from two years ago came calling. Why was it that it was always him? Always that incident at the bar she had never returned to. Why did that particular memory have such a hold on her? To this day, reliving that encounter had the power to completely enrapture her in the feelings and sensations she had experienced. She could still feel his hand crashing down on her rump repeatedly, still feel his fingers thrusting in and out of her before being replaced by his hard cock as it hammered her pussy.

I don't have time for that, she thought adjusting the water from hot to cold. Her body retaliated by squelching any and all need for anything other than a warm towel.

Drawing back her dark, mahogany hair, she pulled on leggings, a hand-knit sweater from a trip to Peru the previous year, and cowboy boots. Native American earrings and necklace completed her outfit and grabbing her shearling jacket, she hopped off her houseboat before running up to the top of the locked gate. The liveried driver was waiting.

"Dr. Montgomery?"

"Yes, good morning."

The poker-faced driver helped her into the car, closing the door behind her. Flynn had to admit she was impressed. It wasn't the usual SUV turned limo; no, this was a vintage Rolls Royce. *Ben should get a kick out of this*, she thought as the driver negotiated the Seattle streets from the marina where she kept her floating home moored to Ben's trendy loft on the waterfront. She smiled. The twenty-five grand she'd received for the sale of the fossilized penile bone had completed the amount Ben had needed for the down payment on his place. He had been worried he might lose it, but her gift ensured he was able to purchase his home.

The Rolls pulled up in front of Ben's building. He came out in what was generally considered the uniform of entrepreneurs in the Pacific Northwest—designer jeans, designer sweater, leather bomber jacket, and expensive boots of some kind or another.

"Looking good, sister mine," he said as he slid in next to her. "Isn't this car gorgeous? I knew Henry Koto had one. I hoped he'd send it for us."

She shook her head, "Boys and their toys…"

"Expensive toy."

"When you're the best, you get all the goodies and trappings that come with success."

"I know, I'm working on it," he said with a grin.

Ben was a hard worker. He had been busting his butt since their parents had died. First to make sure she was provided for and had a great education and then to make a success of what had once been their parents' dream for a family-owned adventure business. Once Flynn had entered college, Ben had joined the Navy and become a SEAL. When he had ended his term of service, he'd gone to work as a marine salvage diver, while starting and making Daredevil Adventures the most sought-after adventure company in the world. They had started small, but each year, Ben garnered a bigger share of the market.

They pulled up in front of the Koto Building and Ben jumped out, extending his hand to Flynn, before the driver could get out.

"No sense in you getting wet," he said holding his upturned hand to the sky to catch the rain in his palm.

He and Flynn headed into the building.

"Mister and Doctor Montgomery? I'm Cheri Atkins, Mr.

Koto's executive assistant. This way, if you please," a cool, patrician blonde said, turning towards a bank of elevators.

They followed her into the glass elevator and Ben reached for her hand. He was probably the only person in the world who knew how terrified she was of the contraption. She could hang off a cliff, secured only by a piton at fifteen thousand feet as though she was climbing up the steps to her favorite restaurant, but glass elevators scared her to death.

The elevator was mercifully fast, and they reached their destination quickly, the doors opening with a smooth swoosh. Executive Assistant Atkins exited, turning towards what Flynn assumed was Henry Koto's office without another word or so much as looking back over her shoulder.

Ben whispered, "It's almost like we are well-trained Poodles and she told us to heel."

Flynn laughed. "No, wrong hair. You look more like a Portuguese Water Dog and I look like a half-drowned Cocker Spaniel."

They were ushered into an enormous corner conference room that was all glass on two sides. Despite the dreary Seattle day, it was overly warm. Naturally, the great man wasn't there. This was all a part of the corporate culture; the lesser mortals were kept waiting for those of more importance. Both she and Ben went to the edge of the room to take advantage of the commanding view.

"Dr. Montgomery, it's a pleasure to meet you," Henry Koto said in a cultured and surprisingly pleasant voice. There was something off-putting about the Koto brothers—not so much their physical looks, but in the way they moved and looked at you as if sizing up whether or not you were worthy of their notice. Most women did not measure up in their eyes and Flynn realized she was no exception when he ignored her proffered hand. "Ben?" he said extending his hand to her brother. "Good to see you again. My brother absolutely raved about the trip he took with you to the Great Barrier Reef."

Ben smiled. "That was a great deal of fun. If I ever find the right girl and settle down, I hope I have a friend like Michael to throw me a destination bachelor party. All five of them seemed to enjoy themselves."

"So much so that we are planning a staff retreat for our executive officers. Cheri is putting together the details. Would you mind terribly if I fobbed you off on her to start planning that? I'm sure your sister can handle any questions I might have."

Knowing that landing Koto Development as a corporate client would be a huge feather in Daredevil Adventures' cap, Flynn said, "What an excellent idea. Multi-tasking at its best."

"You don't mind?" Ben asked Flynn.

"Not at all," she replied, spotting the executive assistant waiting just out of direct sight.

The blonde woman opened the conference room door and ushered Ben out.

"I do hope you don't mind and won't be uncomfortable meeting with me alone. I promise to be on my best behavior."

Flynn turned away from the view and leaned back against the window. "I don't mind at all. If I couldn't handle a billionaire in a business suit, I'd have no business guiding anyone in the wilderness... much less said billionaire."

"Touché and my apologies. In this day and age, I fear I have to be sensitive to anything that could be labeled harassment..."

"Let me assure you, Henry, if you harass me, you won't end up talking to my lawyer. It'll be the business end of my bowie knife," Flynn answered in a lighthearted tone of voice, but they both knew she was deadly serious.

If she was going to take this guy up into the wilds of Alaska, best he learned from the get-go who was in charge... and that it wasn't him. Henry Koto nodded his head in acknowledgement.

"I assume your brother told you about my upcoming

show," said Koto. "The pièce de résistance will be an up-close picture of a Kodiak, without the use of a telephoto lens."

"I'm afraid the only kind of cameras I know anything about are point and shoot. What difference does it make which one you use?"

"There's a difference in the quality of the end result and I would really like the exhibit to be more than just a vanity project."

Flynn was impressed. Henry Koto seemed sincere in his desire to deliver a product worthy of exhibiting in a well-known Seattle art gallery.

"The problem is that this is mating season. Kodiaks on their best days are temperamental, but add in hormones and breeding drive and the situation gets a lot more complicated and dangerous."

"You see? This is why I want you as my guide. Your in-depth knowledge of the species will be integral to my success."

"Henry, anyone with an internet connection can tell you when mating season is. It may well be impossible to get a pass into any of the parks."

"I don't just want any of the parks, I want to go to Shuyak Island."

"Shuyak? Why? It's probably the remotest and because of its size and its Kodiak population the most dangerous."

"I thought it had a small population of bears."

Flynn nodded. "It does and they compete for everything as resources are more scarce. You'd need to use extreme caution and avoid any kind of surprise encounter. Kodiaks aren't warm, cuddly teddy bears. They are the largest and arguably the most fierce."

"Polar bears…"

"Aren't sweet cartoon characters either. But pound for pound, I'd rather go up against a polar bear than a Kodiak. That being said, we can probably make it safe enough if we stick to Kodiak Island."

"No, I have my heart set on Shuyak."

"I'm afraid this may be a case of you not getting what you want."

Henry Koto turned away and took two steps before turning back around. "Are you saying you will only agree to be my guide if I agree to go to Kodiak?"

"In essence, yes. But if you aren't going to listen to my recommendations, then perhaps you should hire a different guide."

"No, that won't be necessary. I would prefer to avail myself of your expertise. Would it be possible for us to leave the day after tomorrow?"

Taking a deep breath, Flynn nodded. This was too easy. Men like Henry Koto didn't easily accept no for an answer. "I assume you and my brother came to terms?"

He nodded in the affirmative.

"Then," she continued, "we'll make arrangements to fly us up to Kodiak. I'll email you a list of what personal items you'll need to bring. Will it just be you and me?"

"Yes, unless that would make you uncomfortable."

"I find my bowie knife to be an excellent companion," she said smiling. "Then we'll make flight arrangements to get us to the island."

"Let me. We have very experienced pilots and private planes are so much easier and nicer than commercial jets. I can have my driver pick you up at… say the same time day after tomorrow?"

"That will work, Henry," she said, extending her hand. This time he took it.

CHAPTER THREE

Alex Kingston plucked the salmon from the icy waters with his powerful jaws. He looked up to see his brother, Joshua, approaching. He tossed the fish at him, hitting Josh unawares.

"Shit, Alex. Knock it off. That water is cold," scolded his brother.

Catching another for himself, Alex slogged up out of the frigid stream. He dropped it at his brother's feet and huffed before shoving his nose into Josh's groin, knocking him to the ground.

"Really, asshole, that's the way you want to play it?"

Alex watched his brother stand and call forth his spirit animal, a large Kodiak brown bear. Only as his twin brother, it wasn't so much a spiritual calling as a true shifting of his physical being. It always amazed Alex that what internally felt like the smooth flow of water ebbing against the shore, appeared to an onlooker to be the merest glimmer of light. One minute there was a 6'4" man on two legs and the next there was an almost 4'6" tall at the withers Kodiak bear on all fours.

Joshua cuffed his brother's head. Were it anyone else, Alex would have taken it as a challenge and defended himself. But Josh was his baby brother, albeit younger by only seven minutes, and this was just standard twin play. Alex charged and bowled Josh over, the two wrestling loudly. Both brothers did their best to defeat the other. Massive paws with razor sharp claws swatting each other as large mouths gaped and grabbed, trying to maul the other into submission. Alex was the larger of the two—as a man standing 6'6" and as a bear standing close to 5'; he was also the more muscular of the two.

Alex had put himself through school, majoring in wildlife studies and law enforcement, preparing himself for a life as a backcountry ranger in the Alaskan parks system. Joshua, on the other hand, had followed a different path, marrying his high-school sweetheart who knew his secret, and becoming an English professor whose courses on cryptozoology were standing room only at the University of Alaska. Josh had just returned from a book tour, promoting his first book. He had been unable to shift for months and it had taken its toll on him.

The two wrestled on the rocky shoreline, each trying to best the other but enjoying the tussle more than actually wanting to win. When they tumbled into the mind-numbingly cold water, it shocked them into shifting back. Joshua's clothes had been torn asunder when he had shifted. That meant that the only clothing to be had was Alex's. Recognizing that fact, the two grown men once again battled as they scrabbled toward the rock where Alex had left his clothing. Alex was the heavier and more muscular of the two. Knocking Josh backwards, he made a dash for his clothing, scooping it up before Josh could recover.

Watching his brother pull on his jeans, Nordic sweater, and mukluks, Josh said, "The least you can do is throw me your parka."

"Why?" laughed Alex. "I'm not the one who got all growly and shifted before taking his clothes off."

"Yeah, but its cold out here and a long way back to your cabin."

Alex lived off the land. The population of Shuyak Island was anywhere between four and ten, depending on the season and who you asked. While he would have preferred to live in a cave as his ancestors had done, being a part of the world meant having to have some kind of address, even if that was a Forest Service cabin in the middle of nowhere with a post office box on Kodiak Island.

"And again, I'm not the guy who wasn't careful with his clothes. I sure hope Allie doesn't get too pissed."

Joshua laughed, his eyes glowing not with the feral light of being a bear-shifter, but with the love he had borne for his wife since they were in high school.

"Nothing I can't romance her out of," Josh said grinning.

Alex shook his head. "That's not our way."

"We aren't true Kodiaks, Alex. You know dad always said our kind mate for life."

"I'm not disputing that fact, but if she were my woman, she'd damn well do as I told her or pay the price for her disobedience," he scoffed.

"Easier said than done, big brother. And unless things have changed, your mate still eludes you in Seattle. I knew when I married…"

"Mated, Joshua. Bears don't marry."

Josh held up his left hand, wriggling his fingers to indicate his wedding band. "This one did, and I knew when I did it that I'd have to make accommodations."

"In other words, go belly-up whenever Allie has a sharp word for you."

Alex liked his sister-in-law, but he thought his brother had long ago given up his status as the head of their household, a common mistake as far as Alex was concerned.

"That's not how it is, and you know it."

"What I know, little brother, is that she has you pussy whipped and wrapped around her little finger."

Josh bristled. "Not true. When you marry outside of our kind, you have to make certain adjustments. Allie still answers to me and I make her toe the line…"

"Is that what you call it when she racks up speeding tickets or overspends on frivolous things?"

"What may seem silly to you means a lot to her. It isn't easy for cheechakos. She gave up a lot to marry me and live in Alaska."

Not wanting to hurt his brother's feelings for no reason, Alex teased, "I thought you made up for that in the sack."

Josh laughed. "I do. Why do you think she's still here?"

"Not for that," Alex said indicating Joshua's genitals that were contracting and shrinking from the cold.

"Gimme that damn parka and we can compare equipment when we get back to your place."

Alex tossed him the warm coat. "You could be in Florida and you still wouldn't measure up."

Josh grabbed the parka and cuffed his brother's head again. "You really are an asshole, you know that?"

"You're right, little brother, I really am."

• • • • • • •

"Have you got everything together for tomorrow?" asked Ben, standing in the living area of Flynn's houseboat.

"I don't…"

"What?"

She stuffed a last pair of wool socks into her pack.

"I don't know. He's been very polite and certainly having him arrange for his driver to pick me up and to use his private plane is nice. There's just something about him and this whole trip that kind of sets my teeth on edge. I know how silly that sounds; it's nothing specific, just something I can't quite put my finger on."

Ben reached out for her, grasping her forearm, and forcing her to stop and look at him. "It doesn't sound silly to me. If you have any misgivings, we can cancel."

"No. That would be bad for Daredevil. He's booking that huge retreat, he's done absolutely nothing wrong, and I can take care of myself."

"I know you can, but if you think there's something hinky in all of this…"

"Nothing I can put my finger on. I'm probably just still jet lagged."

"Flynn…"

"Ben, let it rest. A week, ten days at the most and I'll be back. Maybe I'll get lucky and it'll only be a day or two. The bears should be active; it's mating season."

"Aren't they more aggressive? Is it safe?"

"I should be able to keep him safe on Kodiak. He wanted to go to Shuyak, but I let him know that wasn't happening."

She finished the last of her packing just before ten. She knew Koto's driver would be waiting for her.

"Don't fret. It'll be fine. He'll get his picture. If his show does well, maybe he'll mention us in the credits." She glanced down at her watch. "Do me a favor? Close up the boat for me." She leaned over and kissed him on the cheek. "I'll let you know when we're headed home."

"If you're sure…"

"I am."

"Then stay safe; have a good time and I'll see you in the next couple of weeks. I'll lock up the boat."

She nodded and headed up the boat ramp to the limo. At the top of the rise, she stopped and looked back, waving to her brother.

• • • • • • •

"How long are you here for?" Alex asked his brother.

"Just for a week or so. Allie's never really cared for mating season. And now that we have kids, it's not as easy as it was."

"And again… not our way."

"We'll see what happens if you ever decide to settle down and have kids. Speaking of which… when are you going to find a mate? Oh, that's right; you found her and she ran off, managing to elude you for the past two years."

Alex knew his brother had long given up the hope that he would turn from the old ways and embrace the new as so many of their kind had done. He knew it worked for Joshua and a lot of the other shifters of their generation and those who were coming after him, but it rankled that civilization had so encroached on their habitat that they were being forced to change. Technically, Alex was clan leader, certainly the alpha of what was left of those who lived among the islands located off the coast of Alaska.

"Female Kodiak shifters aren't as plentiful as they once were. Of course, if you'd turned Allie, your daughters would have added to our numbers in due time."

"Allie had enough trouble accepting what I was; she didn't want to be turned."

Alex arched his eyebrow, "At the risk of repeating myself yet again, not our way."

"You think I should have turned her after she said no?"

"I think you should have claimed your mate properly and not given her a choice in the matter."

Josh grinned. "You really are a Neanderthal. No wonder you don't have a mate. I don't even think your attitude would fly with the females of our kind."

"Actually, neither Neanderthal nor asshole. I am Kodiak and clan leader. I will hold to the old ways as long as I can."

"So, you think you're going to find some female you can chase down, claim, and breed with no courting, no nuance, no romance?"

"Courting and romance can come after dominance is established and she has submitted to me," said Alex curtly.

Grinning at his brother, Josh clapped him on the back. "Yeah, good luck with that. I might remind you that you tried that once, and last time I checked you had yet to find her again."

"I will find her."

"It's been two years. Maybe you ought to seek

another…"

"No," growled Alex. "I will find her and when I do, she'll regret having run from me."

Josh shook his head. Alex never visited anymore. Any vacation he took was spent in Seattle hunting the woman he was convinced was his mate. Josh was only able to visit once a year for a week or two when the need to rut was the hardest to resist. Visiting Alex made it easier for Josh as he was not in the proximity of his mate. For a Kodiak, mating season in the presence of his mate meant one thing and one thing only, breeding her long, hard, and often.

Josh was right, though, finding his mate had proved to be elusive. He was loath to admit it to Joshua, but in his own way he was an incurable romantic. Alex believed that at some point he would find his mate and they would live as closely as possible to the ways of their ancestors.

They'd been out fishing and were returning to the cabin. During the Summer, there was never a true night. It was full light from four in the morning to midnight. Further south, they had a few more twilight or darker hours, but the entire region experienced what was called the season of the midnight sun. Conversely, from November through January, it was almost an eternal night. Although Kodiak shifters experienced the instinct and overwhelming urge to mate in May and June, with offspring being born in January or February, most Kodiak shifters found they coupled more during the eternal night with their offspring born seven to eight months later.

"Do you think you'll have trouble this year?" asked Josh.

"Not with humans. I've managed to find a reason to quash any passes to the park or licenses for hunting or fishing. Amongst our kind and the true blooded Kodiaks, things could get a little dicey. For the past few years some of our younger male shifters have taken to mixing it up with the true blood bears. So far, I haven't heard of them trying to mate with the sows, but I worry with habitat shrinking for both species that there could be real trouble down the road."

"What would be the point? We can only turn humans, not true bloods. And have you ever wondered why bears and pigs use the same designations for their males and females? I wonder about these things."

Alex grinned, enjoying his brother's penchant for wandering off topic. "I don't think about that kind of minutia. I do know that there's some talk that maybe it isn't true… maybe we can turn true bloods too. Frustration is at an all-time high and the fact that unlike true bloods we mate for life is becoming an issue."

"Why would they believe some idiocy like that?"

"Strong sex drives combined with a lack of available females can create a lot of tension."

"That's the case all over Alaska where men outnumber women…"

"Yes, but ours is compounded by many feeling human females shouldn't be turned without consent."

"An idea you don't subscribe to."

Alex shrugged. "It's an idea that could lead to the extinction of our species."

"Are you saying that you'd turn a woman if she didn't want to be turned?" Josh asked incredulously.

"If she was my mate, yes," he said nonchalantly.

"Then I'd better never meet her…"

"You mean Allie had better never meet her."

Josh grinned. "That too."

Alex grunted. "Someday, little brother, you may well have to become the dominant partner in your relationship."

"Equal partners works for us."

"Until push comes to shove."

The two twin brothers eyed each other, realizing that at least for now, this was an issue that would not be resolved between them.

They finished cleaning the fish, Josh preparing those they would eat for supper and Alex preserving the rest for consumption later in the year. After dinner, they started a game of chess. The two were fairly evenly matched and so agreed to pause the game shortly before midnight. Alex pulled the blackout curtains over the windows to make the cabin as dark as possible to encourage sleeping and then turned in.

CHAPTER FOUR

Flynn leaned back as the private plane took off, sipping a mimosa that had been supplied by a flight attendant. Perhaps it was the alcohol, but Koto's jet seemed a bit on the warm side. Other than that, she had to admit to herself she was impressed. She'd been in noncommercial planes, but most had been floatplanes, and all had been propeller driven. The smooth speed with which the jet took off along with its luxurious appointments ensured a pleasant three to four-hour flight.

"Do we have an itinerary?' asked Henry Koto.

"I had originally thought of going to Port Lions, but you talked about Shuyak. They aren't giving out any permits or licenses for the island. But Ouzinkie's terrain is more like Shuyak so I thought we'd head up there."

"That sounds good, Flynn. We keep a floatplane up here in Alaska…"

I'll just bet you do, thought Flynn.

"I'll let our pilot know where we're going," said Henry, standing and heading up to the cockpit.

Flynn watched him go. She wasn't sure why just about everything Henry Koto said rankled her, but it did. Normally she enjoyed leading adventure trips for her brother as well as getting to know the clients, but not this time. She didn't like Henry Koto. She just wanted him to get his picture so she could be done with him.

They touched down on the island where an SUV waited to take them to the floatplane. Once on board, Henry's skilled pilot took off and headed toward their final destination, Ouzinkie, which was on the northern tip of Kodiak. Flynn leaned back, not bothering to glance down at the scenery during the short flight.

The plane landed on the water, sidling up to a small dock. Stepping out, Flynn looked around.

Putting her hand on the pilot's arm to stop him from off-loading their gear, she said, "I remember Ouzinkie as being a bit larger than this."

"A private dock belonging to a client," answered Koto smoothly as the last of the gear was off-loaded.

Flynn turned to look back at the shoreline and was startled when the floatplane's engine came to life and the plane moved off.

"What's his hurry?" she asked Koto.

"One of my brothers has need of him back in Seattle. We always try to put business ahead of vacations. I slipped our ride up here onto his schedule between other things."

Although it sounded plausible, there was just something about Koto and the situation that was causing the hair on the back of her neck to stand up.

Hefting her pack onto her back, Flynn said, "Are you sure you want to keep on all those layers? I worry that you'll get overheated. Where are we in relation to the town?"

"I'm fine. I detest the cold. We're due west of Ouzinkie. Do we need to go there?"

"No, I have our permits and licenses, just getting my bearings. I think we should head north up the coastline. Depending on how far we get, we can either camp out on the beach or head inland a bit. This time of year, we could see bear signs here on the coast, but more likely, they will be up closer to the trees by some of the waterways."

They hiked for the next few hours; Koto never removed any clothing and never even broke a sweat. Flynn pointed out various birds and other wildlife, including tracks of various animals.

"Is there something amiss, Flynn?" Koto asked when they stopped for a break.

"I'm a bit surprised you don't have your camera out…"

"I'm only interested in the Kodiak," he said interrupting her. "Why don't we head inland? I'm still feeling pretty strong. Why don't we see if we can't find a spot to set up a base camp?"

Flynn nodded. "We can do that. You know, you seem rather at home up here; I wonder why you hired us?"

"I think I may have fooled you into thinking I'm better than I am," said Koto self-deprecatingly. "I don't mean to step on toes, and your expertise in the wildlife and tracking are well known."

Flynn smiled. "I have on hiking boots; my guess is my toes are safe."

"After you," he said with a sweep of his arm.

Flynn ignored the prickly feeling along her skin as she walked past him and headed up into the trees. They made good time and found a good campsite close enough to the water to have it easily available but off any of the wildlife trails.

"I think this will be good site. There's water relatively close, but we aren't on a game trail. It's flat and this big boulder will lessen the perimeter we have to worry about and will help reflect and hold heat. This is good ground to set up a cookfire…"

"So, you're thinking a base camp and day hikes?"

Flynn nodded. "I am. It's more efficient and a lot easier as you can cover more ground, carrying around less. We can use small day packs and there were plenty of bear signs. If we don't get what you want, we can move to country we haven't covered and set up again."

"You see? I knew I'd picked the right guide."

She extracted one of the fishing rods she'd brought and put it together handing it to him along with a small bait container.

"Do you mind walking down to the river and seeing if you can catch us some dinner? I'll get the camp set up and when you get back, I'll clean the fish and make us dinner. We can come up with a game plan for tomorrow and make it an early night."

Koto took the proffered fishing gear and turned to go.

"Henry? You might want to take a rifle. It is mating season, and this is Kodiak country. You need to keep the gun handy and keep a sharp eye out."

He chuckled. "Right. After all, that's why I came."

He turned and left. She watched his retreating back and started setting up a fire ring. She was moving his pack out of the way when a camera case fell out. Flynn opened it to ensure Koto's equipment had not been damaged. She was no expert, but what she extracted from the case did not appear to be the kind of thing someone would use for photographs to be exhibited in an art gallery. It seemed fairly elemental to her.

She turned back to her own pack, planning to dig out the topographical map she had brought with her. Just as her fingers touched the map, a shot rang out... followed by a strangled and aborted scream.

∙ ∙ ∙ ∙ ∙ ∙ ∙

Alex and Josh had spent several days that seemed to harken back to their childhood as well as strengthen their bond as brothers. Having stopped to have something to eat, they were both stretched out, basking in the sun.

"Allie always fusses at me when I stretch out to catch some rays," said Josh with a smile and a certain wistfulness Alex was used to hearing when his twin brother spoke of his mate.

"It seems to me Allie does a lot of fussing about things

of little importance."

"She worries about melanoma."

"Bears aren't inclined to melanoma."

"While she knows that intellectually, it's hard for her. When I'm with her, I look and feel completely human…"

"Really? Most guys I know don't stay hard for hours unless they have great control and supportive medication."

Josh laughed. "That may be the one part of my being a bear-shifter she does like. The ability to stay harder for longer is something we make frequent use of."

"And yet, it's mating season and you aren't rutting with your mate."

"I don't see you making it with anyone either, big brother."

"That's because there aren't any female shifters here on Shuyak or even on the north end of Kodiak. I didn't get leave this year during the season."

"I wondered why you were available when I called. I thought you had seniority and could get away when you needed to."

"Bill Childers is getting married, so I let him take the time. My plan is to head over to the mainland after you leave and find some receptive girls," said Alex.

"Human or shifter?"

"Doesn't really matter, one pussy is pretty much the same as another."

Josh rolled his eyes. "And therein could be the reason you don't have a mate. Seriously, Alex, don't you want to find a mate?"

"I do, but there are few women—human or shifter—who want to live up here in a cabin on the outskirts of nowhere. I don't think I could settle for the half-life you lead."

"I'm happy, Alex."

Alex clapped his brother on the back. "I know you are. But to not be able to shift on a regular basis… to be human ninety percent of the time just isn't for me. I need this," he said indicating the wilderness expanse. "I'd like a woman who'd be happy at the cabin, but happier up in mom and dad's den."

"Would she have to be Kodiak shifter?"

"Bear shifter of some kind would be preferable so I could rut. But I'm not opposed to her being human and turning her. I never understood why you didn't just turn Allie?"

"We talked about it, but it just wasn't something she wanted or could accept."

"So that means you're the only one in your family who can shift. You could be the last of our line."

"Oh no, you don't get to lay that on me. I know several bear shifters, Kodiak and Grizzly, that would gladly take up with you. If you're so concerned about our line, pick one and get on with it."

"Not for me. Dad always said only take a mate if the thought of living without her made it feel like someone had grabbed your guts and squeezed. And for all the shit I give you, I know Allie makes you happy."

Josh chuckled. "You just think I ought to make her behave."

Alex nodded. "I think there is something very appealing about having a woman over your knee when she's disobeyed you and then taking her from behind so that she's fully aware of who's in charge."

"Jesus, you're such a Neanderthal. How the hell do you know so much about it, anyway?"

"There are a lot of girls, shifter and human, that get turned on by a spanking and plenty of clubs where men with certain proclivities can find them."

"Are you talking about hookers?" Josh asked in a whisper.

Now, it was Alex's turn to laugh. "Why are you whispering? Who the hell do you think is going to hear you? But, no on the hookers. Just some nice places where relatively normal girls go to find a bit of dominance and release the control they normally have to have in their day-to-day lives."

"Well, Allie doesn't like to be spanked."

"If you're doing it to discipline her, she's not supposed to."

"We'll see what happens when you find a mate. All your esoteric theories and fantasies are going to go right out the window."

Alex shook his head. "I know it works for you and Allie, but there's no way I won't be the one in charge. In all my past relationships, I have been."

"The key word in that sentence being *past*," Josh teased. "What do you say we shift and race down the mountain to the stream."

"Sounds good," Alex said, reaching down to take off his boots then realizing Josh had already stripped, grabbed his clothing, shifted, and begun racing away from him.

"And he calls me an asshole," he grumbled, quickly getting undressed and getting his things in a bundle. He spied one of Josh's socks and started to pick it up. *Nope, he can bloody well wear his boots with only one sock.*

Alex shifted and began chasing after his brother. It occurred to him that it was only fair as it seemed Josh had been chasing after him most of their lives. He cleared the meadow and started following Josh's trail, weaving between the trees and through the underbrush. The smell of water drifted up to him and he feared Josh had managed to beat him to the stream, something he knew his younger twin would lord over him for the rest of his visit.

Hearing a shot ring out, Alex made a split decision to remain in his shifted form to cover the distance more quickly. He bounded into a small clearing by the fast-moving creek and saw Josh crumpled on the ground and a man—a hunter—nudging him with a high-powered rifle. His acute hearing allowed him to hear Josh moan and he saw the man take aim.

Alex charged, leaping his brother's prone body and

cutting the man's scream off with one mighty swipe of his paw with its deadly claws. Blood spurted from the man's severed artery, its scent telling him it wasn't human. Its warm gush covered the man's face, chest, and arms. He turned back to his brother, and shifted back to his human form. He leaned down and Josh growled.

"Easy, bro. It's me. Let me see how bad you're hurt. Don't shift until I see how bad it is. You're stronger in this form," he said rolling his brother to his side.

Josh groaned and pointed to a spot behind Alex. Alex knew the man who'd injured Josh was dead; he'd practically decapitated him. Then he heard the sharp inhalation of breath and stood, spinning around to challenge the new threat.

Before him stood a tall, curvaceous, mahogany-haired beauty in boots, leggings, and a flannel shirt. He couldn't believe she was standing in front of him. His mate had come to Shuyak.

"Oh my God," she breathed.

The look on her face indicated she'd seen him shift. He found it curious that while there was fear, there was also curiosity. He didn't blame her; seeing a bear become a man had to be a bit disconcerting.

Before she could turn and run, Alex closed the distance between them and managed to grab the long, curly ponytail that fell past her shoulder blades. Jerking her back into his body, he made short work of ripping the bottom of her shirt, gagging her and binding her hands behind her back. He dragged her over to the dead body and stripped it of its belt, quickly securing her feet and legs and then placing her where he could keep an eye on her while he examined Josh, who was once again human.

Alex probed the wound. The bullet was a large caliber and deep. Josh was losing blood… fast. He needed a hospital and he needed one now.

"Hang in there, Josh," Alex said.

Ripping the shirt off the dead man, Alex again detected

a faint whiff of something not quite human. He tore the shirt in half, wadding up the bottom and pressing it into the wound and binding it with the top half of the shirt, using the sleeve to apply pressure. Josh was drifting in and out of consciousness and groaned, as Alex added a stick to the knot in the sleeves and twisted.

Alex smelled the campfire. "Yours?" he said to the frightened woman, who nodded. "Anyone else there?" She shook her head. "Good girl. You keep doing what you're told, and you might just live to tell the tale."

Alex stood and walked over to her. He towered over her, looking down and sniffing the air, eyeing her speculatively. He ran toward the smell of the campfire, stopping just out of sight to ensure she hadn't lied.

This was going to complicate things; how much had she seen? Sensing no other humans, Alex ransacked the camp, taking what supplies he needed to help Josh and make a travois. He then disguised the resulting mess so it would appear a wild animal had done it. The girl wasn't unprepared, her rucksack included an impressive bowie knife, a stiletto, and a good rifle. He ran back to the stream.

The girl didn't lack heart, she had managed to get herself close to the rifle, but not close enough. Alex swatted her backside. Her muffled yelp told him her thin leggings had done little to protect her.

"Don't do that again," he growled.

He crafted the makeshift drag sled for his brother and got Josh as comfortable as he could. Rolling the man's body in a blanket, he placed it next to Josh. Hauling the girl to her feet, he removed the belt from her legs. She tried to knee him in the groin and missed. He wasn't as lucky at evading her stomping his instep. He quickly grabbed her by the waist and bent her around his hip before his hand connected sharply with her rump several times and she responded with a similar stifled yowl.

"Try it again and I'll use this belt across your ass. Got it?"

She nodded.

"I need to get my brother some help or he'll die. He dies and you can join your friend."

He looped the belt around her neck like a slip lead, picked up the handles of the litter and headed for his cabin. It was remote and he could secure the girl while he got help for Josh and figured out what the hell to do with her.

The going was slow and rough but checking Josh's wound confirmed that he had slowed the blood loss to a trickle and that Josh was mostly comatose. The girl fought him at first, but two sharp yanks and another hard swat and she settled down and fell in beside him.

Once at his cabin he opened the root cellar, created a pallet with blankets for her and locked her inside. He bound her feet, but not her legs. Satisfied that she wouldn't be able to escape, he went into his cabin and radioed for an emergency evac. Once the chopper was on its way, he called Allie.

"Hey, Alex. You two having fun?"

"We were. Josh has been hurt."

"Hurt? How bad?"

"I have a med evac headed in. We'll take him to the hospital in Kodiak."

"What happened?" she asked.

Alex smiled. For all the crap he gave his brother, Allie had been a good choice. Her tone indicated she feared for her husband, but she wasn't devolving into tears.

"Hunting accident. He's been shot."

"Alex? Will he live?"

"I think so. I won't lie to you. It's bad, but I've staunched the bleeding and the hospital will know it's a gunshot wound and will be ready."

"I'll get someone to take care of the kids and join you there," she said, her voice trembling.

"Hang in there, Allie. I'll have someone meet you at the airport. They'll bring you to us."

"Take care of him, Alex. I love him so much."

"I know, Allie. He loves you too. I can hear the chopper. I gotta go."

He disconnected, picked up the poles to the travois, with its heavy burden, and made his way to the meadow with all haste, where the helicopter would have to land. By the time he got there, the medics were waiting with a gurney. They secured Josh and the dead man inside the chopper's fuselage—Josh on one side and the dead man on the other. One of the two-man team stayed to monitor his brother and Alex took the seat up in the cockpit next to the pilot. They were swiftly airborne and headed for help.

"King?" said the pilot, using the nickname those who knew Alex often used. "You've got blood all over you."

"It's not mine." He turned to the man in the back. "How is he?"

"He's been shot, so not good, but all things considered, I think you probably saved his life. What happened to the dead guy?"

"Looks like a bear attacked him. Maybe that's how Josh got shot. I really didn't see anything. Can one of you guys get someone to pick up his wife at the airport? Her name is Allie," said Alex.

"Consider it done."

The medic on board called into the hospital to update them as to Josh's condition and to report they had a dead body. The chopper landed on the helipad, handing his brother off to the trauma team and the body to the morgue attendant.

One of the nurses touched his arm. "Hey, King. Let's get you downstairs and checked out."

Kodiak and Shuyak Islands both had small populations. Those in the Forestry Service and the Emergency Room were well acquainted.

"I'm fine. Brooke. I want to stay close to Josh."

"Well, you have blood everywhere. Why don't we get you cleaned up and then I'll take you to the OR waiting room?"

Alex didn't like being manipulated, but Allie seeing him covered in his brother's blood wouldn't do her any good. He needed to make sure Josh and Allie were both going to be fine. Then he needed to get back to his cabin to deal with his mate. He allowed Brooke to get him examined and cleaned up. She took him to the OR waiting room to wait to hear that Josh would live. He refused to consider any other alternative.

He wasn't sure how long he'd been slumped down in the chair, using his phone to research shifters on the dark web. The not-quite human scent he'd picked up from Henry Koto most likely indicated he'd been a shifter. But the question was, what kind? Knowing that might indicate whether or not a threat to those under his protection—Josh and Flynn for example—still existed. It wasn't as easy as finding information on Wikipedia, but if you knew where to look, it could be found.

He heard Allie call his name. He got to his feet and wrapped her in his embrace when the beautiful blonde threw herself into his arms.

"Do you know anything?"

"Not much. They sent word out that it's taking longer than they'd thought, but that's all I know."

They settled back on the couch and waited until the doctor came out. "Mrs. Kingston? I'm Dr. Sanders. I just left them closing up your husband."

"Is he going to be all right?"

"We won't know for sure for 24 hours, but I am cautiously optimistic. I can tell you one thing, if it weren't for your brother-in-law, your husband would be dead." He offered his hand to Alex. "Good job, King. You saved his life. I was a bit startled when I looked down and basically saw you laying there. I'd forgotten you had a twin."

"Well, he's always been forgettable," he quipped trying to make Allie smile.

He succeeded and she shook her head.

"And he always says that you're too awful to forget." She

looked at the doctor. "Twins."

He chuckled. "As I said, I'm fairly sure he'll make a full recovery. As soon as we get into a room, someone will come and get you."

Allie shook the surgeon's hand. "Thank you and your staff for all you're doing."

They watched the surgeon head back to the operating suite and Alex guided her back to the couch. A state trooper approached them.

"King? May I speak with you a moment?"

Giving Allie a reassuring hug, he said, "I'll just be over there. Will you be all right?"

Smiling, she squeezed his hand. "Do what you have to do. I'll be fine as soon as I see Josh and know he's going to be all right."

Alex joined the state trooper a discreet distance away.

"Barry, isn't it?" he asked.

"I'm surprised you remember me. Can you tell me what happened? The coroner says the guy was attacked by a huge bear, almost tore the guy's head off. We've ID'd him as some rich development guy out of Seattle. Name is," he checked his notepad, "Henry Koto. Know him?"

"Doesn't sound familiar," said Alex. "What was he doing on Shuyak?"

"According to his brother, some guy named David, he was supposed to be on Kodiak Island photographing a bear. He'd hired a guide... a girl. Did you see anyone else?"

"No one, but then I wasn't looking."

"Did they have a permit that you know of for Shuyak?"

"Again, not that I know of. We don't give out permits during the Kodiak's breeding season because both sexes get pretty aggressive."

"Curious. Your office said the same thing. When I checked with the girl's brother, he indicated that she was an experienced guide and wouldn't mix up the two islands. Apparently, she's been here several times."

"Do you know who flew them in? Maybe the pilot

knows something."

"Apparently, it was the Koto's personal pilot. He's flying back up with the brothers. But you didn't see any sign of the woman?"

"I was a little preoccupied with saving my brother's life. I almost didn't bring in the body, but then decided his relatives would want to know. I did use his shirt to stop Josh from bleeding to death."

"Understandable. We know where to find you."

"I'll be here until I know Josh is all right. Then, I'll head back to Shuyak and start a search for the missing girl and either stay to head it up or come back to be with Josh's wife, Allie. Either way, you know how to get in touch with me."

"We do. I hope your brother makes it."

"Thanks, Barry. I appreciate it." Shaking the trooper's hand, he turned back to Allie.

"Everything okay?" she asked.

He nodded. "Everything will be fine."

A nurse appeared, "Mrs. Kingston? Your husband is in recovery, you and King can see him now."

Alex felt some of the tension begin to dissipate when he saw his brother ensconced in a hospital bed, awake—a weak smile playing around his lips.

CHAPTER FIVE

Flynn strained to listen, trying to ensure he had left. She'd barely heard the whirring of the rotors on the helicopter as it came in. Surely, he would have gone with his brother.

She had to get out! What the hell had happened? There had been a gunshot, a cut-off scream, and blood… so much blood. And had she actually seen an enormous Kodiak bear morph from beast to man? And that man. It was the man from the Irish pub; the man who had spanked and fucked her; the man whose memory still had a powerful effect on her. For Christ's sake, the man had tied her up, gagged her and led her by a belt looped around her neck… and instead of fear, all she felt was aroused. It was annoying.

Once she was sure he was gone, she inched her way over to one of the shelves in his root cellar and managed to catch the edge of the gag on the corner and pried it off. That was better; at least she didn't have that dirty thing stuffed in her mouth. Next, Flynn managed to maneuver around to where she found a sharp metal edge and began working on the material that he'd used to bind her hands. It seemed to be taking far longer than it should. Each time she heard something that sounded like a footstep, she moved herself away from the sharp metal and tried to look pathetic. When she convinced herself that he hadn't returned, she'd make her way back to the metal and continue. Once she'd regained the use of her hands, she reached down and untied the bindings around her feet.

Finally, after what seemed like an eternity, she was free... or at least her hands and feet were. She rubbed her wrists, getting the circulation restored. Listening with her ear pressed to the cellar door, she cautiously lifted the ancient, creaking wood and peeked out. She appeared to be all alone.

Sinking back down, she searched and found a weapon... well, actually, it was a shovel, but it had an edge and could be used as an effective club. This time, she crouched below the door and listened before surging upward with her spade in her hand ready to fight anyone who might be there. Anticlimactically, there was no one. Climbing out of the root cellar, she closed the door and then ran back towards her camp.

Flynn arrived back at her equipment location to find that it had been mostly destroyed and strewn all around. Her sleeping bag seemed to be intact as did a pair of leggings, socks, a shirt, and a polar fleece jacket. Getting her bearings, she gathered her things and started for the coastline. She would have to hide close to the boat dock and wait for the plane to arrive. Closing in on her destination, Flynn realized that they weren't on Kodiak Island at all. How had she been so stupid? Henry Koto had taken them to Shuyak Island. *Damn the man.* Granted, he was dead, but that made it even more appropriate. She found a small hiding place in a niche in the cliff. Gathering brush and rocks to conceal both her and the opening, she crawled in and waited.

She made herself comfortable, or at least as comfortable as she was likely to get for a while. What the hell had she seen? A bear becoming a man... and more significantly, that particular man. He hadn't even recognized her! Why did that irritate her so much? Had what transpired between them meant so little to him? Why did it seem she couldn't forget? Was it possible that she hit her head and been momentarily delusional? She reached back and felt the back of her head, seeking an abrasion, cut, or raised bump. Nothing. And why the hell was she thinking about any of this? She needed to focus on getting away from here. She could make sense of it when she was back in Seattle.

∙ ∙ ∙ ∙ ∙ ∙ ∙

King was able to catch a ride on a floatplane that was headed close to Shuyak. The pilot was a friend and offered to drop him and a rubber raft close to the beach by his home. Once he'd disembarked, he headed for the cabin. He'd been gone longer than he'd hoped, but he had ensured both Flynn's safety and that she would be there upon his return. He smiled ruefully, her safety might be assured, but her backside and pussy would pay the price for eluding him the past two years.

Each year he had returned to Seattle to hunt her, choosing different seasons to see if he could pick up her trail. While he had been able to detect traces of her scent, she had managed to evade him. King had tried alleviating his need with others in her stead but had found the encounters unsatisfying. After a few failed attempts to obliterate his need to rut, he had chosen to suppress his instinct. His mate would pay for that when he finally had her beneath him.

The rut had been harder than ever to endure since he'd fucked her in the office of the Irish pub. The need to mate was an overriding instinct in his kind and was made all the stronger once a Kodiak bear had found his mate. He always looked forward to seeing Josh when he joined him on the island, but having his brother as a distraction had been especially welcome the last two years. He smiled; when he recovered, Josh would be happy to hear that he'd claimed his mate. Alex flexed his hand, he intended to put it to good use when he got back to Flynn. Once he had her bottom a deep shade of red and she was begging for his forgiveness, he'd take her to their bed and make up for lost time where fucking her was concerned. Flynn would learn early on what it was to be rutted by her mate.

It was Flynn's face and the memory of her pussy as it convulsed around the length of his cock that he recalled when he would tightly fist it, stroking and squeezing it with vigor. Closing his eyes, he would imagine that it was Flynn who had her hand wrapped around him. It would be her lips he envisioned nipping and sucking at his neck. King had yet to experience fucking her mouth, something he planned to change when he finally took her to mate. He would make use of that hole as well as her darkest sheath.

When forced to relieve his own need, King would fist his cock harder and faster as he felt his balls swell and the semen rise up in preparation to be spewed forth into nothingness, another thing Flynn would pay for and that would never happen again. He planned to use her hard and often. If he didn't empty his cum into her, he would use it to mark her, spraying himself over her back or breasts and rubbing it in so that the scent of his essence remained behind.

He could see Flynn in his mind's eye, on her knees before him, spreading her legs and offering her wet, warm pussy for his pleasure. His fingers would flex involuntarily as he imagined taking hold of her hips and holding her steady while he mounted her and sunk deep. As King imagined her response, he would move his hips in the same rhythm and pace as that set by his hand, fisting himself until at last his release gave way. While pleasuring himself allowed him to keep his need at bay, he vowed to himself that once he had Flynn where she belonged, he would never be pleasured by his own hand again. It would be Flynn's hands, mouth, ass, and cunt that would provide that exquisite gratification.

Shaking his head to break his own reverie, he set a quick

pace, arriving at the cabin in record time. Seeing the door to the root cellar open, and not being able to detect fresh scent, he lifted his face to the sky and roared... the sound reverberating through the hills and valleys.

∙ ∙ ∙ ∙ ∙ ∙ ∙

David and Kevin Koto had been shocked to hear of their brother's death... not particularly saddened, but surprised. Henry was tough and strong; it had made no sense until they heard it was a Kodiak bear that dealt the lethal blow. Tension had been growing amongst the brothers for the past few years. Unlike their father, they had intended to follow the old ways of their kind. In a long-distant past, anyone harming or killing a member of their clutch would be hunted down and killed in a horrific manner. But as they had moved further away from their roots, the distance had diluted most of the bloodlines and many had lost their prominence. The Kotos were one of the last clutches that could claim to be purebloods, never having mated outside their own kind.

Mating had been on the Koto brothers' agenda for the past year. The brothers had located and had been in negotiation to procure a pureblooded female to breed and begin to provide each brother with the heirs and offspring they required. Henry's death had meant that instead of ensuring their newest acquisition provided a satisfactory return on their investment, they had to be in this gods-forsaken ice box tracking down his killer.

As the jet's stairway deployed, David said to his brother, "There's the SUV."

"What the fuck are we doing here, David? Why did Henry insist on this ill-fated venture? There is no economic justification for it. We have a mate en route to Seattle. The mating season started last month, and Henry insisted we all remain abstinent for the last six months. I don't know about you, but my balls are about to burst."

"The female will keep. Henry wanted the bear as a trophy and for its reported aphrodisiac properties. When we kill it, we will have someone extract those things we need from it. It is important that others of our kind understand anyone or anything that tries to harm us will be dealt with in the harshest manner."

"So, we kill the bear. Who's going to care?"

"Not just the bear, Kevin, that guide… that female, Dr. Flynn Montgomery."

"She didn't kill him, the bear did."

"She was hired, in part, to keep Henry safe. She failed. She dies," he said as the door to the SUV was opened and they entered the vehicle.

Kevin shivered. "I thought this thing was supposed to be warm when we got in."

"Incompetence surrounds us, brother. We will persevere." He addressed the driver, "Take us to the hospital and turn the heat up. We have to identify our brother. Keep the engine running. We won't be long and you will need to return us to the airport."

Both brothers sat back and gazed out the window as the SUV sped towards the hospital where they were greeted by the hospital administrator who personally escorted them to the morgue.

Looking at his brother's lifeless body, David asked no one in particular, "And Dr. Montgomery?"

"Who?" asked the administrator, handing David a clipboard with several forms he glanced over and signed.

The brothers exchanged glances, before Kevin replied, "A friend of the family. We are to meet her later today."

David cleared his throat. "As of the cause of death is obvious, can you skip the autopsy and send my brother's body back to Seattle for preparation and burial?"

"State law indicates that we autopsy all unexplained deaths… and the coroner noted a few anomalies in his internal organs," said the hospital manager.

"I'm no coroner, outdoorsman, or even from Alaska,

but I can see my brother was mauled by a bear. Perhaps, you could incorrectly interpret the regulations as being suggestive rather than directive? It would mean a great deal to my brother and me if Henry's body could be immediately cremated according to our customs and readied for our return home. My family would be most generous if the hospital could accommodate us."

He looked the director in the eye; the other man nodded and made a call to a local funeral home to arrange an immediate pick-up and cremation.

"I understand your grief and you're right, there is no question as to the cause of his death and no reason to inconvenience those of you who loved him," he said.

David discreetly wrote out a check for a large donation to the hospital and handed it to him. "Thank you for your cooperation, assistance, and kindness. It is most appreciated."

Having completed the official identification and signed the forms necessary to have Henry's ashes prepared to return with them to Seattle, the brothers were driven to the dock where their pilot waited with the floatplane to take them to the site of Henry's death. They would shoot the bear who killed him, or at least some Kodiak, and track down and take revenge on the female who had been hired to guide him.

"Have you decided how she is to die?" asked Kevin in a casual tone as they stepped out of the plane onto the dock where Henry had been dropped and watched it taxi away.

David smiled, "I thought we might enjoy using her before I bite her and leave her to die alone in the wilderness, terrified of what happened to her."

"Yes, the moment you have them on their bellies and you shift as you lay down on them… nothing quite like it. I always wonder what any forensic team makes of it. But Henry said we should avoid fornicating with lesser people now that we will have a proper mate to breed."

David chuckled. "Doesn't leave the authorities anything

other than clueless. And what Henry wanted or thought is no longer relevant. The fact is, instead of having to share our new mate with two brothers, we shall only have to share with one."

• • • • • • •

Flynn spotted the plane as it landed in the water and taxied up to the dock. She started to rise and step out of her hiding place, but some instinct deep inside her warned her to stay hidden. She shivered but tried to calm and quiet her breathing so as to remain undetected. The two men stood back to back, each of them swinging his head from side-to-side and sniffing the air.

"David, I think I smell her," one of the men said, looking in her direction.

The other man turned in the same direction, inhaled deeply, looking directly at her concealed location and nodded.

"We have her."

Knowing that she was the *her* they were referring to, Flynn ensured she had her knife, rifle, and climbing gear, left her hiding spot and made a break for the forest. She was fairly sure from the obvious newness of their clothing that she knew Shuyak better than they did. She glanced once over her shoulder to see them lumbering after her. Flynn put on a burst of speed and made for the tree line, veering off in a different direction and heading deeper into the woods. Cresting a hill, she looked back. The vegetation was not overly heavy, and she could see them moving slowly, but deliberately along the trail she had made. Not once did they look up or even ahead. They seemed to be watching where they were putting their feet as opposed to looking for her.

Flynn took several deep breaths and set off running again. She wanted to put as much distance between herself and the two men who meant to rape and kill her as she could. She had two advantages: one, she was more experienced in the rough terrain. They weren't exactly clumsy, but their movements were slower than she might have expected and very deliberate. The second thing in her favor was that while she was waiting, she was able to get her bearings and realized she knew the approximate location of the ranger station. Flynn turned in the right direction and made her way, without haste, towards the station.

What the hell had the guy meant when he said, the moment you have them on their bellies and you shift as you lay down on them… Shift? Shift into what? What fucking rabbit hole had she fallen down?

• • • • • • •

King was making his way towards the camp that Flynn had set up for her and Koto. He didn't expect her to be there, but it was as good a place as any to start. If he couldn't find any sign of her there, he'd backtrack towards his cabin and pick up her trail.

As he approached the tent, he slowed and scented the area. She wasn't there now, but she had been earlier. Flynn was long gone. He found the freshest tracks, studied them and followed. It didn't take long, or a genius, to figure out she was headed back to the dock where presumably the plane bringing her and Koto to Shuyak had dropped them off. He quickened his pace. He meant to ensure she didn't escape him again.

Reaching the beach by the dock, his nostrils were assailed by a scent he didn't associate with the island. It wasn't immediately identifiable, but its memory tickled the edges of his mind. He could, however, detect Flynn.

He found the place she had hidden away. He smiled, his mate was intelligent and cautious. Alex recognized the pungent scent of urine where Flynn had been. He realized that was the scent he had picked up from Koto, and that he had just detected. The hackles went up on his neck…

something or someone had peed all over the area. Whether to disguise her scent or as some kind of warning or retribution wasn't clear, but in either case, it did not bode well for Flynn.

Without bothering to undress, King shifted, destroying his clothes. He needed to get to Flynn as fast as he could and the best way to do that was to call forth his bear and go after her and those who were in pursuit of her. His sense of smell was amplified when he was in his Kodiak form and he could travel faster. He was running, pushing his endurance and lung capacity to cover the ground. His mate was in danger and he needed to eradicate the threat to her.

• • • • • • •

Flynn thought she was making good time. She was trying to balance being careful over the uneven, rocky ground strewn with half-buried roots with increasing the distance between herself and her pursuers. She came to a swift-running waterway that looked treacherous to cross. She scanned the bank and spotted a large boulder on the far side. Perhaps her rope would be long enough that she could tether one end around the rock, driving her knife into the ground on this side to secure the other end of the line.

She knotted a loop and swung the climbing cord like a lariat, trying to get it to reach around the rock. She missed several times—the makeshift lasso wasn't quite long enough to reach easily if she created a large enough loop to easily encompass the stone tower, but too small a coil and she wouldn't be able to get the rope in place. Finally, she found the balance between the size of the noose and the length of the cord. Success!

Flynn was just finishing adding rocks to secure her knife in the soil by the stream. Just as she was picking up the stretched lead, her two pursuers burst through the brush and rushed her clumsily. Flynn crashed into the water, holding onto her guideline. It was taut and the two men seemed reluctant to enter the water. She didn't blame them, it was freezing.

Suddenly, she felt the rope come loose and turned to see they had cut it. It slipped from her hand and was swept away by the current. Flynn had to catch her balance and secure her footing before she could move.

She heard something big entering the water, too big to be one of the men. Carefully, she turned to see something that looked like a large, low-slung dinosaur coming towards her.

"Hurry, Kevin, don't let her get away. We can build a fire for you when you get her out."

Please, God, let me be dreaming, she thought. This couldn't be happening. First a Kodiak had killed Henry Koto and then somehow morphed back into a man and now some giant lizard was trying to catch her. The only problem was that lizards were not indigenous to Alaska, nor could they survive long in its harsh climate. She needed to wake up from this nightmare!

She had slipped when she turned, dropping her rifle and her foot was now lodged between two rocks. She was as effectively trapped as if her limb had been caught in a steel trap. The creature was closing in and she could do nothing but watch. To add to the danger, a large, seemingly aggressive Kodiak bear charged onto the beach. The only other human in this terrifying scenario raised his rifle and fired, the shot only grazing the large beast, who rushed by him, swiping at him with one deadly paw as he did. The man went down as the bear hurtled himself towards the thing pursuing her. She leaned down trying to free her foot as the beast turned to face the threat from the Kodiak.

Managing to get loose, Flynn made her way through the thigh-high deep water, slowly but surely.

• • • • • • •

Hearing the voices of the two men ahead, King forced

himself to pick up the pace. Just before he cleared the foliage, he remembered where he had smelled that scent before. The one from Koto, left by those in pursuit of her and in the urine. It had been on a trip with his nieces to the Seattle zoo. Somehow, there was a Komodo dragon hunting his mate. Komodos were not found, outside of zoos, anywhere other than Indonesia, which meant that the two men pursuing her were shifters.

As he hit the beach, he saw one man on the riverbank and a large Komodo wading into the water to get to Flynn who appeared to be stuck. He barreled toward the human, who took aim with a high-powered rifle and fired. King was able to maneuver just enough that the bullet only grazed his shoulder. He swatted the man with his enormous paw as he stampeded past him, splashing into the water and grabbing the giant lizard by the tail, pitching it away from Flynn.

The beast twisted its body and made a grab for his jugular, which was protected by thick fur and a large layer of fat. It was painful and he could feel venom pumping into the wound. He knocked the dragon's head loose, submerging it in the water and standing on it, feeling it give way as it was crushed against the bottom of the river. King glanced over his shoulder and saw the man on the side of the river, gaining his feet and making a grab for his rifle.

King raced towards Flynn, who had freed herself and was trying to make for the other side of the fast-moving water. He ran in front of her, blocking her way. He nudged her with his muzzle toward his back. She didn't understand. Gently, he took her arm between his powerful jaws and directed it to the top of his back before kneeling into the water so that she could climb aboard. She seemed to understand and clamored up onto him with a leg on either side of his massive shoulders, grabbing his fur in tightly clenched fists. King got to his feet and bounded to the opposite side of the river from the man with the rifle. The trees were closer on this side. He made his way toward them in a zigzag pattern. The man fired his gun again and missed them completely before they made the relative safety of the woods.

He loped towards a spot in the forest that angled up and would give them a good vantage point. The shot that had almost missed him had apparently been deeper than he thought but was already beginning to heal. As he ran, the pain increased but he was able to ignore it more and more and focus on the task at hand. He needed to put enough distance between himself and the hunter to provide them with a certain degree of safety. King also wanted to find a spot where Flynn would be unable to flee from him easily. He rather imagined she had a number of questions, but he had a few of his own. Why was she being stalked by Komodo shifters? Did she know who they were? And why had she run from him two years ago?

CHAPTER SIX

Flynn had a death grip on the coarse fur of the bear that had saved her and was carrying her far away from the violent scene to which she'd been a witness. She had to focus on hanging on as the great beast lumbered along a path that seemed known only to him lest everything that happened overwhelmed her. She'd always known Kodiaks were enormous creatures but sitting atop him gave her a new appreciation for just how immense they were in sheer size.

She was trying to process all that had happened in the past hour. She'd heard two men plot to rape and kill her— two men she knew to be David and Kevin Koto, Henry's brothers. But what had happened to Kevin… had he somehow morphed into the Komodo dragon whose skull was crushed by the bear on which she was riding? She clung to the bear, trying to ward off the wave of dizziness that washed over her. Had someone slipped her some kind of drug that was causing her to have continuing hallucinations? Was there any hope at all she might wake up to find she was in her own bed on the houseboat having just returned from New Zealand? Or had all that had transpired somehow been initiated by the night in the pub? The beast scrambled up the side of the mountain, moving swiftly through the heavy brush and trees until it entered a small cavern and once again knelt down.

Flynn slid from its back, noting that the bear was blocking her exit. It stepped back creating a bit more space and then seemed to shimmer before her eyes, as if it and the immediate air surrounding it… It? Him? All of the edges of the bear seemed to soften as if smudged before the entire outline disappeared only to have the process reverse. When the shimmer faded, leaving only the hard edges of flesh and bone, it wasn't a bear that was on one knee, folded over himself. Before she could extend her hand or see if he was in pain or needed assistance, he stood. There was no question as to the gender of the beast… the fully erect cock that jutted away from his body was all the evidence she needed to attest to his sex. Her eyes were riveted to it and for a fraction of a moment she recalled, all too well, the feel of it stroking in and out of her sheath—nothing had ever felt more sensual, more dominant, or more right.

"Flynn," he growled—the sound seeming to reverberate in her bones, before freeing all the butterflies in her belly and below. "Are you all right?"

She was silent for a moment until she recovered her voice.

"All right? I'm so fucking far from all right I don't even know where to start…"

Before she could finish, the beast growled again, a low, reverberating sound that skittered along her skin, causing her nipples to stiffen and her pussy to pulse. He reached out, grasping her upper arms before pulling her into his hard, naked body. No, this couldn't be happening again. Her mind, what was left of it, knew she should resist, but she had ached for him for so long and lust from the adrenaline surge was coursing through her veins.

He tore her clothes from her body, removing her boots and socks so that she was as naked as he was. He reached up to heft the fullness of her breast, pinching her nipples as he did so. He inhaled sharply. Knowing that Kodiaks had an intense sense of smell, Flynn was fairly sure he could detect her arousal. If not, her beaded nipples and moan, as he'd run his hand down her side cupping her buttocks while continuing to fondle her with the other, would have been a dead giveaway. The need to be possessed by this man, to feel his strength chase away the fear, clouded her ability to think rationally.

Spinning her away from him, he shoved her over to a large boulder in the cave, placing her hands on the rough surface and pulling her hips back before kicking her legs apart. With no further warning, two of his fingers invaded her pussy, roughly stroking her. The noise he was making was not human, nor was it wholly animal, but some kind of hybrid in between. All she knew was that no other sound had ever spoken to the deepest part of her and called forth a profound need to be dominated and possessed by this man… this beast… this whatever the hell he was.

Lust, in its most pure form, spread throughout her body like a wildfire out of control. She remembered all too well his feral coupling and craved it like an addict needing a fix. The last rational part of her brain cried out for her to say something. But that part of her amygdala that appeared to be in control silenced any protest she thought to make.

"I have missed you, mate," he growled as his hands dug into her hips.

He mounted her in one powerful thrust, forcing her interior walls to stretch in order to accommodate his size. He rammed home, the tip of his staff reaching the end of her sheath as the rough texture of the rock scraped her delicate skin. The weight of his body pinned her down. There was nothing refined or gentle about his possession. It was brutal and primitive, his need inflaming hers. His body demanded hers submit to him and it answered in primal surrender.

"No," she wailed as she climaxed around him.

"Yes," he hissed as he pulled back and rammed home several times before beginning to thrust within her with long, hard, deliberate strokes.

In the same way he had morphed from beast to man, she felt as though she was transforming from woman to a creature that needed this primeval, hedonistic claiming as much as he did. The animal between her legs pounding her pussy was in complete and utter control as he fucked her, and she reveled in his domination.

Flynn offered him no resistance, none whatsoever. She merely responded to him as she had in Seattle with repetitive orgasms, each more intense than the last. She could barely breathe and gasped as his cock hammered her cunt relentlessly. She needed to feel his strength and power. Only then could she wallow in his rough possession and stifle any misgivings she might have about being taken in this manner, either now or in the past. The sounds he made as he drove into her repeatedly were neither fully animal nor human but lay somewhere in the realm of fantasy. He grumbled and groaned as he plundered her pussy until, at last, she felt his release was imminent. Flynn felt his cum begin to gush into her as his cock jerked within, twitching and pulsing as her pussy's contractions from her last climax caressed his cock.

Her need for him assuaged, reason returned to the fore. She wanted to feel ashamed or violated for having allowed him to claim her with none of her questions answered and with fewer words spoken between them than when it had happened in Seattle. Flynn couldn't understand why she had responded to him in the abandoned manner she had. Never had she experienced what this man was capable of making her feel. She had all but convinced herself that the first time was an anomaly; that would no longer be the case. She knew that this had been no mere coupling to satisfy the lust that often accompanied intensely dangerous situations. Something within her understood it had been his declaration that she was his and that she would surrender to his dominance and need to possess her.

When he finished, he uncoupled from her, running his hands down her back and pinning her back down when she tried to rise.

"You stay where I put you, whether that's in a root cellar for your safety or bent over something after I've fucked you."

"My safety," she scoffed. "You and I both know you left me there so I wouldn't contradict whatever story you told the authorities. Who are you? No, scratch that, what are you? And how the hell aren't you dead? You were wounded and then bitten by a Komodo dragon."

"No. My Kodiak physiology makes me impervious to bacterial infections and venom. The wound was fairly minor and has almost healed. Again, due to my being a Kodiak shifter. Now, you will answer my questions. Have you been injured and why did you run from me in Seattle?"

"So, it was you," she breathed.

"You know it was. Now answer me," the growl had deepened and there was a definite edge to it.

"Where do you get off making demands of me? And now after you've fucked me a second time without my consent you bother to ask if I've been injured? How the hell would I know? You kill whatever that… that thing was, scoop me up out of the river and drag me up here so you can get your rocks off. No, I'm not even close to all right. We have a brief, albeit intense, encounter two years ago in a pub when I didn't know you were some kind of freak, then you kill my client… that was you, right?"

"Yes. He tried to murder my brother. Why were you up here helping a guy on an illegal trophy hunt for a Kodiak?"

"I didn't have any inkling he wasn't up here to do anything other than take pictures until right before all hell broke loose. He didn't shoot a bear as far as I could see, and I only have your word he tried to murder your brother. Considering the enormity of what I don't know about you, I think it's a bit much to ask me to give you the benefit of the doubt. And where did you get off spanking and fucking me in the first place two years ago?"

He chuckled—a deep, seductive sound that launched

her libido back into the stratosphere.

Flynn told herself it was simply the residual adrenaline reaction to the danger she'd survived.

"Interesting how you keep coming back to our first time. I would take that to mean that you understood the enormity of our meeting. Now, either you answer my questions about whether or not you're injured and why you ran from me or the spanking you get for putting yourself in harm's way will get a whole lot worse. Which would you prefer?"

"You'll what?"

"You heard me, Flynn," he said evenly.

He crossed his muscular arms across his brawny chest covered with tawny-colored hair that was heavier across his pecs and then tapered off as it ran down the center line of his body past his navel, acting almost like an arrow pointing at his engorged phallus that had the vestiges of his cum combined with hers covering it. He stood tall and proud and seemed unaffected by the fact that he was stark naked in front of a woman he barely knew. Flynn was finding it difficult to divert her gaze from his impressive appendage.

"You don't get to talk to me that way," she said lamely.

"Oh, but I do. First you bolted on me in Seattle, then you managed to elude me each time I came looking for you…"

"You came back to Seattle looking for me?"

"Why does it surprise you that I would come after my mate?"

"I'm not your mate," she said incredulously.

"You are," he stated flatly.

"I'm not. I'm just a girl that let you beat her ass before tossing her over the edge of a desk and fucking her to the point she was sore for days afterwards."

He quirked his eyebrow and nodded towards the stone.

"Alright, and put up with your rough treatment earlier. But if you let me go and swear never to bother me again, I won't tell anyone about you and will just go home and leave you in peace."

He laughed, but it was not a sound that held any mirth. "First, you didn't *let* me do anything," he said. "I spanked you in Seattle so that you would understand from the get-go that I would dominate in our relationship and that you would submit to me in all things. It's a common enough practice amongst my kind. The fact that you didn't take that lesson to heart was obvious when I returned to take you out of that bar to find you gone. I had thought to preserve some of your modesty and pride by leaving with you through the back entrance. I won't make that mistake again. Second, as to you being sore, you'll have to get used to being fucked more roughly and routinely than you've been used to. After a while, though, I will probably only make you ache either when I choose to or during the rut…"

"The what?" she asked surprised at the matter-of-fact tone he was using. "I don't know what you are or what you think is going to happen… and I am grateful for what you did back at the creek…"

"Had you not been so elusive, none of what has transpired in the past few days would have happened. Josh wouldn't be lying in a hospital and I wouldn't have a minor wound. Third, you might want to take a more amenable tone with me as you're lucky I don't have a strap to welt your ass with me and will have to settle for using my hand."

"A strap?"

"Yes. A belt can serve the same function, but I think having a strap that hangs by our bed might help you to focus on why you want to behave. Are you injured?"

"What? No, I'm not injured, other than the scrapes and bruises my latest encounter with you will, I'm sure, produce. Do you hear yourself? A spanking? A strap? Fucking me hard? In addition to being an arrogant prick, what the hell are you and for that matter, what was that thing you killed in the river and what was David Koto doing there?"

Flynn could feel herself getting hysterical and tried to rein in her emotions. What had she allowed to happen? She could excuse the first time in Seattle; she hadn't known what he was, but this time she knew… maybe not yet what he was, but that he was not human. Although, the cock that he'd hammered her with had felt decidedly human.

He moved towards her and she recoiled. A deep rumbling came from his chest that was somehow soothing and comforting. He reached for her and grasped her upper arm and prevented her retreat.

"Enough, Flynn. I'm not sure we lost Koto; we should get on the move."

"Oh sure, we can stop long enough for you to fuck me, but when it comes to giving me answers I need, we don't have time. I've got news for you… I'm not going anywhere with you."

"I wasn't asking, Flynn; I was telling. Are you going to come willingly?"

With the arm that he hadn't been holding, she'd been reaching behind her, searching for something she could hit him with. She had to get away. Her fingers found a rock; she swung it towards his head with all the strength and speed she could muster, but his reflexes were well- honed, and he ducked out of the way.

"Nasty-tempered female," he said, pulling her into his body and wrapping her around his hip. "I would have preferred to wait until I had us in a more secure location, but I don't have time to debate what we need to do."

She could feel his cock beginning to stiffen as his hand came down with a resounding crack. The sound seemed to bounce off the walls of the cavern, eerily echoing all around her.

"You bastard," she screeched as the pain in her ass reached her brain.

His strong arm held her in place as he swung his hand down and landed agonizing blow after agonizing blow to her backside. Feeling her flesh respond to the impact of his hand was deeply painful and oddly arousing at the same time. She could feel her pussy pulse each time his hand connected with her buttocks. Flynn yowled and squirmed, trying to get away from him.

The creature, whose name she realized she still didn't know, proceeded to cover her buttocks with hard swats. She could feel the pain and fire blooming all across her rump as he spanked her.

"You will learn to mind me, Flynn. The longer you fight me, the longer your spanking will last. Keep in mind that regardless of how long this takes, I'm going to expect you to move at a fairly quick pace until I decide we are safe."

He spanked her to punctuate each word. Flynn couldn't believe this was happening to her. Her ass hurt… a lot. The beast continued and seemed in no hurry to stop. Repeatedly he struck her bottom; she wailed in response, twisting and turning, but failing to free herself. He held her in place bent over his hip and spanked her with the only sound being that of his hand walloping her behind.

The worst part was as much as it hurt, she could feel her nipples forming stiff peaks and was quite certain if he didn't stop, her pussy was going to start dripping all over him. She was dismayed at her wildly out of control response to him. This was the second time he had spanked her as well as the second time he had fucked her without any attempt to seduce her or ask her permission. Flynn had the distinct impression that in both instances, he felt his actions were justified and realized, at least on some level, that she had never been more aroused. The feelings of discomfort and desire continued to increase and warred within her.

The wicked blows all along her backside compounded to increase the level of heat and pain she was suffering. She tried telling herself that whatever it was that had driven him to claim her sexually and spank her, and her acceptance of both, was beyond either of their abilities to stop it from happening. Perhaps that was true for her, but he seemed completely in control of himself. Biting her lip, Flynn tried to keep from crying out and begging him to stop. Recognizing that she was unable to free herself or force him to cease, she admitted to herself she could endure no more.

The silent tears quickly developed into crying and pleading which devolved into great, heaving sobs.

"Stop, please, stop! I'll go with you. I'll do what you want. Just don't…"

His hand seemed to stop mid-swing as he brought it down gently to rest on her agonizingly sore posterior. She tried stifling her tears but found it difficult to do so. He set her on her feet and handed her the sweater that he had stripped her of. He ripped what was left of her jeans into strips, braiding them into two strands, one much shorter than the other. The shorter length, he used to bind her hands together. The second he looped through the bindings around her hands and then wound the end around his fist. Leaning down, he picked up her boots, tied the laces together and slung them over his shoulder. He headed out of the cave and gave what was effectively her leash a little tug.

"At some point you're going to have to answer my questions."

"But that time is not now. Keep up or I'll cut a switch to use on the backs of your thighs to ensure you do."

"Ok, but can you at least tell me your name? I mean, you know mine; it would help if I knew what to call you."

He stopped for a moment, turned, and seemed to consider her request. "Kingston, Alex Kingston. Most of my friends call me King."

"As we aren't friends, I'll call you Alex."

He smiled. "At some point, my very beautiful mate, your bottom will thank you to consider what tone you take with me."

"I am not your mate," she said belligerently.

He tugged on her leash as he turned and resumed in the direction he'd been going. They walked for several hours in complete silence. Alex seemed to be mindful of the fact that neither of them had on shoes. He stopped once at the crest of a hill to look back down, his gaze sweeping across the landscape below.

"Can I ask where we're going?"

"Home," he said.

"Won't David Koto think to look for you there?"

"Doubtful. My cabin's location is not well-known nor is it easy to find unless you're a park ranger, but even if he could find it, we won't be there."

Flynn stopped, digging in her heels. "I demand you tell me where you're taking me."

Alex did not respond except to push aside several twigs of foliage before breaking one off and stripping it of its leaves. He jerked the cord he'd created with her torn jeans until she was pulled up next to him. He switched the backs of her legs, two on each thigh. Flynn yowled.

"Come," he said before taking up the lead and hauling her along behind him.

They continued up the hill. When they reached a cliff-like area, she balked as he started up the rise covered with shards of shale. He turned to look at her, anger beginning to cloud his eyes.

"My feet aren't as tough as yours. Can you slow down so I can sort of pick my way along?"

Without a word, he approached her and slung her over his shoulder.

"For Christ's sake, I don't need you to carry me. I just need you to slow down a little bit. Put me down!"

His only response was to swat her bottom, which had been bared and upturned when he'd tossed her over his shoulder. Flynn yelped as Alex continued up the side of the mountain. She closed her eyes as she realized he was tromping along a barely discernible trail, where one misstep would send them hurtling down the cliffside.

Setting her down on smooth rock, he fisted her leash and led her into a small cave. She had to bend over to get in and was relieved when after a half mile, there was a sharp turn as the spacious cavern opened up into a converted kind of open-concept living area, containing a large and ornate iron bed, a sofa and two chairs around a hand-crafted stone fireplace that had a cooking pot hanging inside it, a cookstove, and what she assumed was some sort of bath.

Propelling her into the room, he rolled an enormous, thick wood door into place and pushed it back into the opening like a cork in a wine bottle.

"Won't someone see that and figure out there's something hidden away back here?"

"Not unless they get close enough to see and feel that it isn't merely the back of the tunnel."

"I would think the wood is a dead giveaway."

"The other side is covered in stone," he said, lighting the fire in fireplace.

"The smoke?"

"You are safe. You are my mate and I will lay down my life to protect yours. But if you are truly concerned about the smoke being seen, it goes through a series of filters and is dissipated long before it even gets to ground level."

"So how long do you plan to hold me captive?"

"You are not my captive; you are my mate, and you have known that since Seattle."

Flynn sighed. "You say potato… you want to try and explain what the hell is going on? What the hell you are? Where the lizard came from? Why you seem to think you can beat and fuck me any time you choose?"

"Let me answer your easiest questions first. I will spank and mate with you whenever I see fit. During the rut, I will expect you to alleviate my need. And I will see to yours as well. I suspect the lizard," he chuckled," as you so charmingly named him, was one of the Koto brothers. Given his size and strength, that was no lizard, that was a Komodo dragon."

"How?"

"In the same way I am Kodiak. We are not wholly human…"

"Like a werewolf or vampire?"

Alex smiled. "Not exactly. As you've seen, we can shift at will and aren't some hideous mutants, we are either wholly human or wholly our other being. Shifters have existed as long or longer than those of you who are wholly human. When the world was far less civilized, our ability to shift from one form to another as needed was natural selection at its finest. It allowed us to thrive in environments that would have killed those who could not."

"Like the frigid cold up here in Alaska. And the rapid healing?"

He nodded. "Our enhanced genetic immunity lends itself to being able to recover more quickly and live longer."

"Do you think Henry and David know Kevin was a shifter… is that what you call it? Does your brother know?"

"My brother is my twin. And shifters are not some kind of anomaly in my family. Josh is also Kodiak…"

"Meaning, Henry and David are both Komodo dragons?"

"Yes."

"Then wouldn't the cold bother David?"

"My guess is they have to take precautions against our frigid weather."

"Maybe he'll just go home," Flynn said hopefully.

"Not likely. Komodo dragon clutches are close-knit. You run afoul of one and they won't stop until you're all dead. At some point I'll have to kill the last one."

"How can you talk so casually about murder?"

"I don't see it as murder; I see it as keeping you safe. The remaining brother blames us for the deaths of his brothers. It's a choice between whether I kill him or he kills us."

"What about your brother?"

"I need to get word to him as soon as I get you settled in here. He needs to know they were Komodo and at least one of them is still living. He'll need to ensure his family's safety."

"There will be no settling me. I have a life and I mean to get back to it. It's not that I'm ungrateful…"

Alex growled and yanked her into his embrace, his mouth capturing hers as his tongue swept through her mouth, enticing her tongue to duel with his as arousal flared throughout her system.

"It is not your gratitude that I require, Mate. And your life is now here with me."

His hands ran down her body, fondling her backside and making her wince. He released her and produced a hunting knife, freed her wrists, and rubbed them to restore all of the blood flow and feeling. He turned away from her and entered the bedroom area, opening an antique armoire and withdrawing a pair of padded handcuffs that were linked together by a piece of chain. Flynn ran back to the door trying to dislodge it.

"You are not strong enough to open the door. I will deal harshly with any foolish escape attempts on your part."

"No," she wailed as he locked her wrists in the restraints and the other end around one of the posts of the iron bed.

"I need to get word to Josh and want to reconnoiter the area. You have enough length to get to the bathroom and I will leave food and water next to the bed. You will be safe and remain here until I return."

"You can't just kidnap me and hold me against my will."

He chuckled. "I believe, my mate, I have already done that. Your place is at my side, on your back or belly beneath me or kneeling in front of me. While I am gone, you might try to settle yourself with the idea that you will submit to me. Keep in mind that normally at this time of year we'd be in full rut, so I am having to check that instinct in order to deal with this mess you created."

"Mess I created? If anyone is innocent in this whole mess, it's me."

"You brought a trophy hunter to Shuyak during the rut?"

"I was told it was for a photograph and Koto brought me here on his private plane. It was supposed to be Kodiak Island. Then you kill him, making me a target, and I end up having to try and keep his brothers from killing me, get chased by a giant lizard and get kidnapped by some kind of mutant who thinks it's his God-given right to beat and fuck me whenever he wants."

Alex nodded. "I think you covered all the essential facts except one."

"What did I miss?" she challenged.

"You are my mate and you initiated all of this when you ran from me two years ago. Had you remained at the pub, all of this could have been avoided. As I said, I will clean up the mess you created."

He turned to leave her, effectively chained to his bed.

"Aren't you going to get dressed?"

"No, once I have sealed you in, I will shift back to my Kodiak form. I can do what I need to do more effectively that way. I'll shift back to make the actual call. You will be safe and comfortable while I'm gone. When I return, we'll mate, and I'll feed you."

"We'll mate? You'll feed me? Really? Don't count on it! You don't just announce that you're going out and when you return you plan to fuck me again."

Flynn cried out as his hand snaked out and swatted her backside before crushing her against his body, his quickly hardening cock throbbing between them as he bent her back, exposing her breasts to his rough handling. He nuzzled her neck as he pinched her nipple…hard.

She yowled again but more from frustration than pain. Flynn was mortified as she felt her other nipple quickly tightening and beading up in erotic response to what she assumed passed as fondling for him. His eyes never left hers and he smiled, letting her know that he too had noticed her response. Gaze locked on her, he leaned down and grasped her taut peak between his thumb and forefinger and squeezed it with the force of a vise clamp. Arousal surged through her body, racing through her system as a pool of desire swirled in her lower belly and spread downward, engulfing her nether regions. Flynn's fear was that her sheath would begin dripping onto his staff while at the same time, the nub at the apex of her legs pulsed, trying to entreat his touch.

The smug grin that spread slowly across his face told her it was too late; he already knew of her shame—despite his rough handling, she was more turned on than she had ever been in her life. He reached down and tugged hard on her clit, making her catch her breath and bite her lip to keep from climaxing. He repeated his corrupted form of foreplay, using her nipples and clit as tools to master her body. Then abruptly he stopped, lifted her in his arms and tossed her onto the bed.

"I think, my mate, you will be more than ready for me to mount and rut upon my return. You are not to alleviate your own need."

"How would you know?" Flynn challenged.

He looked at her levelly and growled quietly, "I will know and will make you regret a wrong choice."

Picking up the knife, he opened the entrance to the cavern and disappeared through the opening. Flynn watched as the door to her prison slid back into place, sealing her fate.

I got news for you, buddy. I'll be long gone by the time you get back, she thought.

And why the hell had he left naked—why leave her with that visual? Why had her eyes taken in every bulging muscle, each sculpted plane of his body and his rigid cock? And why, oh why, did the memories of having that cock thrusting inside her have the power to make her shiver with renewed desire?

Flynn tugged against her restraints. She had not expected to be able to easily free herself and she was not disappointed. If she was going to get away, escaping from the handcuffs was her first priority. She had nothing with which to pick the lock so looked for a way she could dismantle the bed itself to at least untether herself.

CHAPTER SEVEN

Reassuring himself that the entrance to his real home was secure and that Flynn would be safe, he put down his favorite hunting knife and called forth the great Kodiak that resided within him. He shook his head trying to erase the images and memories of Flynn. He needed a clear head and his mate was a distraction. He picked up the knife to carry in his mouth. He made his way carefully down the cliffside, ensuring that no sign of his passing was left behind.

Once on the relatively easy terrain at the base of the cliff, he galloped back towards his cabin. There were things there he needed to do. The first thing he did was backtrail to where he had found Flynn. He found the spot the remaining Komodo had realized his tolerance for the cold was fading and that he had lost his quarry. Alex knew that didn't ensure their safety. Komodos were known for their relentless pursuit of revenge and the deaths of two of his brothers meant the last of the three, David, would not stop until he had slaughtered Flynn, her brother, his brother and family, and lastly himself. David Koto was about to find that while not as vengeful as Komodos, Kodiaks were inordinately protective of their families and Alex would ensure that both his family and Flynn's were safe.

Alex turned towards home and picked up his pace. He was able to make good time and arrived before what in the lower forty-eight would have been sunset. At this time, in this part of the world, the sun still shone brightly. That would be one more thing that Flynn would need to get used to—the extremes of the seasons. In the summer, it was almost continually daylight and in the winter twenty out of the twenty-four-hours were night.

Finally, he arrived home, unlocked the small box under his bed that contained his satellite phone and made two calls. The first was to a long-time family friend and fellow clan member, Yutu, who would keep Josh and his family safe. The other was to his brother at the hospital in Kodiak.

"Hello?" Josh's voice sounded surprisingly strong.

"Josh, it's good to hear your voice."

"Alex, where are you? What happened? Allie said you seemed to depart pretty abruptly."

"In a nutshell, Henry Koto brought Flynn…" started Alex.

"Your Flynn?"

"One and the same."

"How'd she get involved with Koto? And what's any of it got to do with my being shot?" asked Josh.

"Koto got Flynn up here under false pretenses. He told her he was looking to shoot a photograph; what he really wanted was to shoot a trophy. He's the one who shot you. When I saw you crumpled in the river, I attacked and killed him. Flynn heard the shot and saw me shift."

"You were going to have to tell her sometime," said Josh wryly.

"Yes, but I'd planned something a little more subtle than having her see me damn near rip a guy's head off. Once I knew you were mostly out of the woods, I had to get back to her."

"Back to her?"

"I didn't have time to explain anything, so I left her bound and gagged in the root cellar."

Josh chuckled, "Oh, this just gets better and better…"

"Not as funny as you might think. I got back to find she had escaped. By the time I caught up to her, the two remaining Koto brothers had tracked her down and the younger one was within striking distance to kill her."

"Why? I mean I'd understand coming after you, but why Flynn?"

"They hold her partly responsible. Besides, Komodos aren't known for being overly forgiving," Alex let that sink in.

"Komodos? The Kotos?"

"Yes. We need to get you, Allie, and the girls to safety."

"Where's Flynn now?"

It was Alex's turn to chuckle. "Handcuffed to my bed up in the cave."

Josh laughed, which quickly became a groan. "Don't make me laugh, it hurts. You left her handcuffed to your bed? I'm guessing not at her request or even with her consent."

"That would be correct. I need to get back to her. I needed to get word to you and get some supplies, but I need to deal with Flynn and get her settled."

"You think you're going to convince her that she's your mate and needs to give up her life to be with you?"

Alex growled low. "What I know is that she is my mate and will be with me. She will need to accept that."

"Good luck with that. It is so obvious that you've never lived with a woman. You may have to compromise…"

"That is your way, little brother, not mine. Flynn is my mate and will submit to me. But she is safe from Koto. We need to ensure you and your family are the same. I've contacted Yutu. He's gone to collect Allie and the kids. He'll get you released and up to the clan lodgings."

"Other than dealing with Flynn, what are your plans?"

"I'll see if I can't broker a peace with the last Koto, but if not, I'll have to deal with him."

"Alex, you're talking about killing a man," whispered

Josh.

"No, Josh, I'm talking about safeguarding my family— Flynn, Allie, the girls, and you. If that means David Koto has to die, I've got no problem with that. The alternative is unacceptable."

There was silence on the other end of the line before Josh sighed. "You're right, of course, but I hate that it all falls on you."

"Part of being the eldest and clan leader. Yutu is going to get the word out to the rest of the clan and our kind in general. He should be there shortly with Allie and the kids. They'll keep you safe and let you heal. I'll try to keep in touch, but don't be alarmed if you don't hear from me for a while." Alex heard the sound of people entering his brother's hospital room. "Josh?"

"It's ok, Alex. It's Yutu with a doctor in tow. You know how to get hold of me. Take care of Flynn and stay as safe as you can. Komodo dragons, huh?"

"Yeah. If he wants to fight, that lizard physiology is going to have a tough time of it."

"Not to mention that they have a pretty high profile so them just disappearing would be problematic."

"Just another unsolved mystery. If it traces back to the wilds of Alaska, maybe those who are not experienced in harsh wildernesses will stay home. Not the worst outcome."

"I suppose you're right, and they have left us with little choice."

"Not us, Josh, me. Flynn is my mate; it's my problem."

"They tried to kill me first… it's our problem."

"We'll leave that argument for another day. Go with Yutu and stay safe."

Alex hung up and dialed Koto Development in Seattle.

"Koto Development. How can we assist you today?" the polished voice on the other end of the phone answered.

"I need to speak to David Koto," responded Alex.

"I'm sorry, Mr. Koto is unavailable, can someone else help you?"

"He'll want to talk to me. Let me speak to his assistant."

The phone was suddenly filled with classical music.

"Kelly Adams. I'm Mr. Koto's assistant. How may I be of help?"

"You can tell your boss that Alex Kingston wants to meet. If he's unsure of who I might be, tell him we met briefly at the river on Shuyak."

Without another word, he hung up. He looked up the number for Flynn's brother's company and dialed.

"Benjamin Montgomery, Daredevil Adventures. Where can we take you today?"

"Ben, my name is Alex Kingston—Alex or King to my friends. Your sister has gotten herself into a spot of trouble up here on Shuyak…"

"Shuyak, she was scheduled to go to Kodiak. Is she all right?"

Alex suppressed a chuckle. He rather imagined Flynn believed she was anything but all right, but he also didn't think Ben would want to hear the particulars about his past with his little sister or his plans for her future. Down the road, he thought Ben would be all right with the idea as his sister would be happy, but until he got Flynn settled, she might be disinclined to reassure her brother.

"Your sister is safe, and I will keep her that way. But you could be in danger," said Alex calmly.

"I'm in Seattle—how much danger could I be in?"

"How much do you know about your client Henry Koto? More specifically the Koto brothers?"

"Where's Flynn?" Ben demanded.

"As I said, she's safe. She and I ran afoul of the Kotos. Apparently, the news hasn't reached the lower forty-eight… Both Henry and Kevin are dead, both at my hand."

"What happened?"

"Henry wasn't looking for a photograph. He was looking for a trophy."

"Shit. I should have known…"

"Not necessarily. I had to kill Henry in order to save my

brother who was accidentally shot. My belief is that Henry would have finished Josh off and turned on your sister," he improvised. "When Henry's two younger brothers came looking for revenge, Kevin attacked and was killed in the ensuing fight. David fired at us, but we were able to get away…"

"You need to take my sister and go to the authorities."

"That would be redundant. I'm the head ranger on Shuyak; I'm the one it would be reported to. You can call 907-555-4400, ask them to verify my identity." Alex gave him his identification number. "I'm concerned that David Koto will be looking to get at Flynn through you—either by hurting or killing you in retribution or to get her to expose herself so that he can get to her. I won't allow that to happen. I've ensured my brother and his family are safe. I would like to tell Flynn her brother is safe as well."

"You're serious. I appreciate you wanting to keep Flynn safe, but getting Flynn to do anything she doesn't want to can be difficult."

"I am serious, and I won't be giving Flynn a choice about her safety," Alex assured him. "Do you have some place you can go? I think being in two locales is probably better as it doesn't give him a single target."

"That's not a bad idea. I could revisit the Hebrides…"

"Too isolated, but the northern hemisphere is probably better than the southern."

"How about Reykjavík?"

"That might be a good choice. Enough population and cold enough that he won't want to go hunting there."

"Wouldn't he just send someone?"

"Not from what I know about them. This is a kind of blood feud and he'd lose face if he didn't handle it himself. If he wants to take over for his brother, he can't afford to do that."

"I can reach you and Flynn on this phone?"

"Yeah, but we'll be out of touch for a day or two. How about we set our watches for Zulu time and touch base in

48 hours."

"Sounds good," said Ben, the reassurance evident in his voice. "And King?"

"Yeah?"

"You take care of my baby sister."

"You know?" Alex asked with humor in his voice.

"Some of it. I had heard some guy was poking around asking about Flynn. So, I did a little snooping around of my own. Want to fill me in on the details?"

"Your sister and I got involved a couple of years ago; she got spooked…"

"Afraid of commitment?" teased Ben.

"Not hardly…" Alex said in a surly tone that bordered on a growl.

Ben laughed. "Her, not you. Look, King, I can call you King, right? I love my sister to little bitty bits, but I am not blind where she's concerned. Flynn has never played by anyone's rules and after whatever happened with you took place, she got really gun shy and seemed to shut down that side of her personality that needs to find that one person who completes you, the other half of your soul, if you will."

Alex snorted. "And you are her polar opposite… an incurable romantic."

"Nah, not incurable… hopeful and patient. You planning to break my sister's heart?"

Alex stopped short. He had always thought of Flynn as his mate, pure and simple. No need to dress it up in lace and ribbons, just her yin to his yang. Their hearts had never entered into it and yet when Ben asked him the question, he was as sure of his answer as he was that the Aurora Borealis would come each winter in a dazzling display of light, pattern, and color. He always believed that their reappearance each year held the promise of magic.

He chuckled. "Far from it. She'll be safe with me. You have my word."

"That's all I need. Forty-eight hours, we check in with each other. If contact is missed, we try again at forty-nine.

If still nothing, we head to the other's position. Agreed?"

"Agreed," said Alex. "You'll be in Reykjavík and we'll be on Shuyak. Head to the main ranger station. Ask for Yutu and tell him who you are. He'll make sure you have back up."

"You aren't just going to hole up somewhere with Flynn, are you?" asked Ben softly.

"Much as I'd like to, I think Koto will be after her and he won't stop until one of them is dead. It won't be Flynn."

"Good. You and I are going to get along famously as brothers-in-law."

Once again Alex was bemused that the idea that he would marry Flynn, as opposed to simply taking her as his mate, had the same rightness as everything else about her. He grinned; Josh was going to love this… and would never let him live it down.

"I believe we will. Be careful, Ben. Koto is powerful and looking to get even. I think there's little he wouldn't do."

"I can take care of myself. I'll be safe enough in Reykjavík. I have friends there. The kind of friends that have your back whether it's legal or not. You take care of Flynn… and Koto."

Alex disconnected the call and put together a small package of things they would need—ammunition, clothing that could suffice for Flynn, as well as a high-powered rifle with a sniper's scope, wrapping them in oilskin so he could easily carry them in his mouth when he shifted to his bear form. He needed to get back to Flynn. For one thing, he needed to ensure she was safe and still at the cave. For another, his cock ached reminding him it was the time of the rut and she was his mate. Besides, he suspected, a well-sated Flynn would be easier to deal with.

He exited his cabin, locking it and adding his keys to the pouch. Shifting back to his bear, he picked up the bundle and made his way back to his home lair.

• • • • • • •

Using the interwoven links of the handcuffs as a kind of make-shift wrench, Flynn worked for hours dismantling the parts of Alex's headboard that would allow her to extricate herself from being tied to his bed. Once freed, she examined the cuffs again. However, they interconnected, they would not be easily opened. She examined the restraints where the cuffs met the length of chain and could see no easy way to separate them. No matter, the chain might come in handy as a weapon and as a means of belaying herself down the side of a hill.

Freeing herself had proven more difficult and time consuming than she had imagined. She found a pair of his sweatpants and fashioned a length of leather lacing to make them fit. She added a pair of his wool socks, her own boots, a clean flannel shirt, one of his sweaters, and a parka. It wasn't glamorous and it wasn't ideal, but it would do.

She approached the massive door to his dwelling. She managed to wriggle between the enormous stone and the wall of the cave. Flynn braced her back against the cave wall and placed her hands and feet along the edge and pushed. Nothing. She changed positions, putting her back against the barrier and pushed against the interior of the cave with her hands and feet. Nothing, not even the slightest budge.

Third time's the charm, she thought. She wedged herself between the rock and the wall. This time, she pushed against the wall with her feet and the obstruction to her freedom with her hands. She had almost given up when she felt the very heavy object begin to give. Finding new strength, she almost wept when she felt it begin to give way.

Her momentary tears of joy turned bitter as the door rolled away from her, she lost her footing and fell, only to be caught by Alex. He was stark naked and fully aroused. He bent down and retrieved a small key from beneath a rock by the opening.

"Your brother sends you greetings and made me promise I would keep you safe. I will keep my promise to him… and to you."

"What promise? You made me no promise. You threatened me about seeing to my own need, but I wasn't all that horny and spent my time more productively by freeing myself," she said lifting her chin in defiance.

"You may have managed to untether yourself from the bed, but that is all you accomplished."

"If you hadn't showed up, I would have been long gone before you returned."

"No. You would never have been able to move the stone door. I can barely manage it and I am far stronger than you."

He unlocked the handcuffs, once more freeing her hands. The instant his back was turned, Flynn looked around for something heavy to grab and hit him over the head with. As she looked wildly around, he rolled the door back into place and then turned to stare at her.

"I spoke with your brother today. He is going to Reykjavík. He and I have set up a schedule to check in with each other. And what I promised you, mate, was to rut with you upon my return."

"I am not your mate."

"You are and more than that, you know you are. Get naked and climb up onto the bed. Stay on your knees and stretch your upper torso down. Spread your legs and—"

Flynn's hands had finally found one of the iron spindles from the bed. She grasped it with both hands and whirled around, swinging it at his head. He batted it away and used the inertia of her swing to toss her face down onto the bed. He clutched the back of the sweater and shirt, ripping them from her back with one, powerful downswing, before tearing her leggings from her body as well. Alex raised her lower body off the bed, cradling her against his chest. He used his other hand to remove her socks and boots. Within moments of his return, he had her naked and on her belly in the middle of his bed, precisely where he'd wanted her for the past two years.

Alex hauled her up onto her knees, locking his powerful

arm around her hips so that she had no choice but to stay in position. She tried kicking out at him, but trapped as she was in such an awkward position, it was ineffective at best.

Flynn had no doubt what he had in mind. After all, he'd been naked when he reentered the cavern and his staff had been standing at full attention. Seeing it again had caused her mind to flash back to the last time she had felt him thrusting inside her… filling her… scraping her inner walls and creating such incredible sensations. Flynn could feel her nipples beading, her sheath pulsing and knew that when he mounted her, he'd find her drenched and more than ready.

"No," she cried, fingers digging into the bedding and trying to crawl away from him.

"Yes," he growled, parting her legs and stepping between them.

"You are not going to do this to me again."

He chuckled. "Oh, but I am and will make you revel in your response to me. You should know that when we are in the throes of the rut, your need to be fucked will be as desperate as my own. I will not be content merely to fill your cunt with my seed, but will fuck your mouth sending it deep into your belly and your ass. You are mine, Flynn, and you will submit to me in all ways."

Alex traced the cleft of her ass, teasing her dark rosebud only for a moment before continuing downward to finger her swollen and wet vulva. Drawing his hand back, he swatted her pussy rapidly with a stinging strength that took her breath away. She squirmed trying to free herself, but it was no use. It was clear the beast meant to use her… and that some part of her wanted him to do so.

Flynn yowled in frustration and pain. The strikes had not been as harsh as those he had delivered earlier to her backside. They were painful and added to the heat and arousal already spreading throughout her feminine parts. He fingered her lower lips and penetrated her wet heat, growling appreciatively when he found her more than ready.

Standing with his feet firmly planted on the floor, he

leveled her hips in alignment with his cock and surged forward, sinking to her depths as her body embraced his possession in orgasmic bliss. Her body shuddered as he thrust within her, grunting and groaning as he did so. He allowed her no time to recover as he plunged in and out, her body arching in a primal response to his claiming.

Alex was in complete and utter control, her body merely the willing receptacle of his lust. He continued to plow her furrow with his mighty staff. He stroked her hard, long, and deep—his pace being sustained through her rapidly cycling orgasms, each more intense and devastatingly emotional than the last. He crashed into her, the tip of his cock feeling as though it hit her cervix with each surge forward. Gradually, his control seemed to erode, and his stroking became more frenzied.

He grasped her hips harder and drove into her. Flynn's body was rocked by the power of her response to him. She was unprepared for her body's ability to recover only to begin the process of climaxing again without any respite being offered. She moaned as he continued to drive into her, causing her to orgasm repeatedly. It didn't take long for Flynn to lose herself to the physical sensations he continued to elicit from her and to lose count of how many times she came.

At last she felt his cock becoming further engorged as it filled with his cum. It felt as if it had doubled in size as he rammed into her, sinking his shaft as deep as he could get it and waiting for a moment. Then, his cum began spurting into her, coating and bathing the ravaged walls of her pussy. He didn't move at all, just held her tight against his pelvis while his cock pumped his seed deep into her body. Her sheath pulsed in time to his release so that it too worked to catch his semen as deeply within her as it could. When at last he had finished, he withdrew and let her body fall to the bed.

Without a word, he turned back to the door, picked up the pouch he had with him and walked to the table and chairs and unpacked.

CHAPTER EIGHT

Alex breathed deeply, the smell of his mate and the aftermaths of his coupling with her were intoxicating. One more reason to kill the remaining Koto brother… he was going to have to take time away from rutting Flynn to deal with him.

"That's it? You just walk in the door, strip me naked, swat my pussy, and fuck me?" she accused.

He turned back to find she had pulled herself into the middle of the bed and drawn her legs up to her chest.

"What would you have me do, Flynn? Woo you with flowers and sweet words? You are my mate and have known so since I took you the first time in Seattle," he answered calmly.

"I know no such thing. If I thought that I wouldn't have fucked so many guys after that."

Alex growled. The idea of another man touching her, much less having bedded her caused his anger and his staff to rise. Before either got the better of him, he recalled her brother's words that she had shut down that side of her personality after their initial coupling two years previously.

"Careful, Flynn, the idea of another male having touched you after I laid claim to you is intolerable and most likely would result in his death. Kodiaks are profoundly territorial, and we don't share our mates. Besides which, according to your brother, you haven't been with anyone since we were together."

"That's irrelevant and my brother has a big mouth. Which brings me back to one of my previous questions… just what the fuck are you?"

"I thought we covered that. I am a Kodiak bear shifter."

"Can your kind breed with humans?"

Alex laughed. "I would think that was apparent, but if not, my cock is already getting hard again and I will breed you more thoroughly to make sure you understand. Are you so enamored at the thought of being bred again?"

"You are a first-rate bastard, you know that? Obviously, I'm well aware that you can fuck me. What I meant was, should I be worried that we had sex unprotected?"

"Nothing to worry about one way or another. If you do not conceive from our last few breedings, you will in the future. Don't fret about it; I will rut with you both during, and I suspect, outside of the season."

"You can't possibly be so delusional to think that I want to fuck you, can you?"

"Whether or not you want to mate is of very little importance. Your body indicates you are of like mind, and your screams of ecstasy have filled this den. You are mine; it is mating season and I will rut with you. Given my response to you, I suspect that I will spend most of the year rutting with you. I find your response most enjoyable."

"Would you listen to yourself? I got news for you… I'm not Goldilocks and I'm not looking to spend any more time in your bed."

"I probably won't confine our mating just to the bed, but make no mistake, where I make our bed is where you will be."

She shook her head. He wasn't sure if she truly didn't understand her new role in life or was just being difficult. Most likely, it was a combination of both. He watched as she took a deep breath and tried to calm herself.

"I really need a straight answer from you. Can your kind get my kind pregnant?"

He leaned back against the table, crossing his arms to regard her coolly. "Yes. Even if you were to remain human, you could successfully bear our children."

"*If* I were to remain human?"

He nodded. "Unlike my brother Josh, I want my mate to be one with me in all ways, so you will need to transition to Kodiak. I will wait until the end of the mating season to turn you as the transition can often take a few days in which I would be unable to breed you. As I have waited more than two years to be able to rut with you, I am unwilling to do that. You have kept me waiting, mate; it has not been pleasant for me."

"What the hell are you talking about?"

"What part are you questioning?"

"Everything? What do you mean transitioning to Kodiak? And regardless, you might want to ask me how I feel about that, or about you, or about being your personal fuck toy."

Alex nodded. "I see. You fail to understand that you have little to no say in the matter. I have claimed you and you will submit to my authority. I have no wish to have a human mate, so I will turn you." He chuckled, "As for my personal fuck toy, I rather think you enjoy that as I have yet to breach your cunt and not find you wet and willing."

"You can't just decide you're going to transform me into some kind of freak," Flynn cried with a note of hysteria in her voice.

"Not a freak; a Kodiak shifter. You will be stronger, better…"

"Better than what?" Her voice was climbing higher.

"Calm down, Flynn. You will be fine. The transition isn't particularly dangerous or painful…"

"Now you're worried about inflicting pain on me?"

Alex was confused. "I have never hurt you."

"You think being spanked isn't painful?"

She was going to have to reconcile herself to the fact that Kodiak society was heavily male dominated, and females were often kept in line by their mates' use of spanking and other physical means to exert control. It was the way their kind had always operated. Alex had often wondered if it hadn't made the females of their species stronger and more resilient.

"If done as punishment, it should be. If it isn't, I'm not doing it correctly, but that is different than my doing something to hurt you. When you misbehave, I will discipline you to correct your behavior. If merely spanking you proves ineffective, I will incorporate other and possibly more severe measures."

"This isn't happening to me," she whispered. "I need to wake up from this nightmare."

"You aren't dreaming, Flynn. Our kind has always lived alongside humans."

"But you're insisting I won't be human any longer…"

He nodded. "I am. I would have preferred if you were Kodiak born, but it is of little consequence. I am clan leader and my mate will be Kodiak."

"Does your kind not like humans?"

"We don't all feel the same and most of us don't paint all humans with the same brush—there are good and bad… just as there are good and bad shifters. My brother Josh's mate is human. They are married as it was important to Allie. While our kind normally have a bonding ceremony, marriage has never been a tradition. However, if you would like to be married in addition to the bonding ceremony, I will indulge you."

He watched with curiosity and humor as her panic and fear fled and her anger rose.

"How very chivalrous of you," she said sarcastically. "You arrogant prick. What makes you think I'd marry you or have a bonding ceremony? I would never say 'I do.'"

"In a bonding ceremony, it wouldn't matter. Kodiak

females are often resistant to being bonded to their mate. If you choose not to say 'I do' for a wedding, we simply won't have one." He raised his hand to try and stave off her objection. "I am alpha and clan leader, no one will challenge me or question my taking you to mate."

"Clan leader? Just how many of you are there?"

"You'd best get used to the idea that it's how many of *us* as you will soon be one of us. And our clan is relatively small. Some clans have entire towns, but we are spread out over the whole Aleutian chain. Of the thirty-five hundred Kodiak bears, only about one hundred of us are shifters. We rarely get together except for bonding ceremonies, before and after mating season, and war councils."

"War councils?"

He nodded. "Yes, if I can't deal with Koto or the Komodo tribunal gets involved and goes after others of our kind, I will call a war council and we will deal with them."

"Won't the clan hold me or my brother responsible? Or maybe both of us?"

"No," he said shaking his head. "Neither of you knew about us nor have you done anything wrong to start the violence. Henry tried to kill Josh and I killed Henry. If anyone is responsible, it's me, which is why I would prefer to handle it on my own and not involve the entire clan."

"Afraid they'd be pissed at you?"

"Not at all. But it is *my* family and *my* mate the remaining Koto will be after…"

"You don't know that. Maybe he gave up and headed back to Seattle and won't bother us again."

"Not a Komodo. They don't give up… ever."

He eyed her speculatively, his cock beginning to ache in addition to being hard. Alex smiled, realizing he no longer had to repress his need to rut with his mate. She was here, she was naked, and he wanted her.

• • • • • • •

Flynn watched him approach. There was a dangerousness about Alex that was difficult to deny, but instead of frightening her, it only served to arouse, entice, and intrigue her. He didn't so much walk across the room to her as stalk. She had the definite feeling that he was predator and she was prey. He seemed very comfortable being completely naked with a tremendous erection.

"On your back, Flynn," he ordered.

"Is that your idea of foreplay?" she quipped.

"There will be time for soft words and gentle caresses in the future. During the mating season, I will mount you whenever I choose."

The words had no sooner left his mouth than he reached the bed and shoved her onto her back. Grasping her thighs, he pried them apart and stepped between them. His cock was fully engorged; dragging her close, he drove into her core without any further preliminaries.

"By the gods, I missed you," he groaned.

As she had the last time, she climaxed simply from his penetrating her. It was infuriating, and yet she couldn't seem to resist him. There was something primitive and feral in him that called to some deep, dark place inside her she hadn't known even existed, but now that it had raised its head, it was like some ravenous beast demanding to be fed.

"Alex," she moaned, not knowing if she wanted him to stop or fuck her that much harder. She feared it was the last.

He held her up so that only the upper portion of her body remained connected to the bed. She didn't have the leverage needed to get away from him. Impaled on his staff, all she could do was writhe. He held her parallel to the bed and perpendicular to his body so that he could stand as he plunged in and out of her, bucking his hips so that his hard rod hammered to the very depths of her being. Flynn climaxed quickly a second time; she was exhausted from their earlier session and thought he could sense that she was almost spent. Alex thrust rhythmically and powerfully, coaxing an additional orgasm from her before increasing the strength and speed so that he found his release in her, groaning as he did so. Flynn cried out a last time as they came together, and he filled her again with his essence.

Alex withdrew from her and held her ankles together further aloft so he could deliver three stinging blows to her backside.

"You do not try to evade me when I choose to fuck you. Do it again and I will ensure that your punishment is severe enough that you don't try it a third time."

"Third?"

"Yes, once in Seattle and just now."

He dropped her legs and turned away. Flynn thought seriously about kicking him or trying to harm him again.

"I brought you some clothes. If you behave, you can put them on while I'm gone."

"Gone? Where are you going? When?" she asked, hoping to keep the enthusiasm out of her voice.

He turned and silenced her with a single look. "Do not think you can escape in my absence. When I return, I will expect to find you naked and in our bed… awaiting me and my use," he growled.

"And exactly how am I supposed to know when you are going to deign to honor me with your presence?"

"When the door is moved out of the way…"

"What? I'm just supposed to tear off my clothes and leap into bed? You weren't kidding when you said no kind words or any kind of foreplay." She shook her head, wondering again if and when she might wake from this awful, but incredibly erotic, dream. "Just so I'm sure I understand. You expect me to sit around, wait for your return and then, when I hear the door open, throw myself onto the bed and spread my legs?"

"If you find it difficult to comply, I'll leave you naked and handcuffed to the bed."

"Bastard," she hissed.

"Mate," he corrected, eyeing her speculatively.

Fearing she had pushed him too far, she verbally

retreated. "This isn't easy for me, Alex. You're asking me to accept a lot of things that are completely foreign to me—the very fact that your kind exists, that another kind of… you called them shifter?"

He nodded.

"…shifter exists and it mostly likely wants me and you and our families dead. What if Komodo dragons have strong ties like Kodiaks… could a war spread beyond just the two species? Could humans become involved?"

"Doubtful. One thing all shifters agree on is that having humans know of our existence would bring about chaos and violence against our kind."

"You don't know that for certain."

"History would tend to indicate the chances are more likely that we are correct than not. I will take it as a good sign that you do not see being my mate as foreign or something that you can avoid."

"Why do you want a mate who doesn't want you?" she cried in exasperation.

He chuckled; she wasn't sure which was more grating, the fact that he found it amusing or the sound itself.

"For one thing, it is difficult to believe that a woman who orgasms just from being mounted doesn't want me on some very deep level. For another, as I said, female Kodiaks can be cantankerous and obstinate about being bonded to their mate. As clan leader I have stood witness to more than one vow being forced from a female when she chose to repeatedly challenge her mate."

"Forced? How could someone force a vow from another?"

"They aren't tortured if that's what you fear."

"I'm not afraid of you," she said lifting her chin defiantly.

"I know. It is your fear of your own feelings and knowing that I am right that frightens you."

"You're delusional."

"You will take your vows and your place at my side."

He turned his back and put together a bundle with clothing, ammunition, sat phone, and food. He wrapped the bundle around the working mechanisms of a high-powered rifle he removed from a locked gun cabinet.

"If you're interested, there is a record of our clan over by the bookshelf. You can read it if you like. You have enough food and water here in our home to see you through several days. If something happens to me, a friend of mine will know and will ensure you are safe. I would spend this time reconciling yourself to your new life."

"Because you think I have no other option?"

"David Koto is dangerous."

"I can take care of myself... been doing so without your assistance my whole life."

"I saw how well you were doing when his brother was closing in on you in the stream. Regardless of the Kotos, I knew you were my mate the first time I bent you over that desk and took you. I've returned each year to Seattle to look for you. Now that I have you, I will not let you go. The *only* way you will be parted from me is death."

"I can arrange that if need be."

"You see? You have the spirit of a Kodiak all ready. Our clan will be happy to see their alpha has chosen a mate who will bear him strong and vigorous offspring. Make peace with your destiny, Flynn. Fighting it will prove painful, humbling, and ultimately futile for you."

In less than a blink of an eye, he dragged her into his embrace, slanting his mouth down on hers and kissing her in a way that left her breathless. A small part of her brain still told her to resist, to at least form some token protest. But the greater portion capitulated to the onslaught of her emotional and physical response and melted into his muscular frame, moaning as she wrapped her arms around his neck and returned the embrace. His hands moved lower, one pinning her body to his as the other fondled her buttocks before slipping his finger between her cheeks and teasing the tightly puckered rosebud.

She managed to separate her lips from his, "No," she whispered.

"Yes, Flynn, in time I will use all you have to offer to ease my lust. Rest while I am gone. When I return, the mating season will have begun in earnest…"

"You mean this isn't your idea of earnest?

He shook his head. "It is only the beginning of the season. The need to breed has yet to fully claim my being and become my highest priority. As it is, I have had to suppress the instinct that tells me to seal you in our den, keep you naked and aroused and fuck you until we are both spent. Your need for me will grow to match my own. The only time when you will be sated is when I have exhausted you and you succumb to sleep. So, take what reprieve you can. When I return, I will be in the full grip of the rut and will have been without you for days."

Alex picked up the bundle and headed to the entrance of the cave. Opening the door, he stepped through and slid it back into place without saying another word. She watched as her only way out was blocked. He had been right; she wasn't strong enough to move the stone out of the way. Taking a deep breath, she looked around the interior. There had to be another way out. Someone as careful as Alex would not leave himself without a means of escape… she just had to find it.

CHAPTER NINE

Alex pushed the rock back into place and brushed away any evidence from the ground that even hinted that the stone was anything other than part of the cavern's wall. There had been a time Kodiaks did not need to disguise their dens. They had once lived free of all societal constraints, but hunters and others had grown bolder and now encroached in all areas of their territory. His clan was known as the Unangan Clan. They were more fortunate than most as their home territory in the Aleutian Islands was still only sparsely populated and infrequently visited by tourists.

His cock throbbed. Barely an hour had passed since he'd spilled his seed in her and his need for her was almost overwhelming. He was certain that if her life wasn't in danger, nothing would keep him from rutting with her. He smiled as the images of the times he had already had her drifted past his mind's eye. There was no doubt that his mate had a passionate streak a mile wide and that in years to come she would welcome the rut… as would he. No longer would it be something he had to endure, but rather something to revel in. Poor Josh would have to find someone else to distract him if he was unwilling to force the issue with Allie.

His musings regarding all of the ways he intended to indulge himself with Flynn were interrupted with the reason he was not between her thighs thrusting his cock into her wet heat. David Koto. Alex planned to call the Kotos' headquarters to try and reason with the man. His goal was to warn him off. If that proved unsuccessful, Alex intended to hunt the man down and dispose of him before he could hurt anyone under his protection—Flynn and her brother, Josh and his family, or his clan members.

Flynn… even thinking of her or allowing his inner voice to say her name evoked very primal feelings where she was concerned. He smiled as he thought that while he wanted her to be safe, he liked the idea that she would challenge him and he could take her over his knee and spank her bottom until it was red and heated to the touch. He found he rather enjoyed pummeling her pussy afterwards with his pelvis slamming into her tender backside. The fact that he had yet to not find her wet and willing left him in an aroused and irritable mood that he was being denied time with her due to having to deal with the immediacy of the threat from Koto.

Reaching a high point on the island, Alex shifted to his human form, dressed, and called Koto Development.

"Ranger Kingston? My name is Cheri Atkins. I am Mr. Koto's Executive Assistant. "

That was different, the last woman who had identified herself as his assistant had been named Kelly.

"I understand you need to speak to him," she continued. "May I inquire as to the nature of your request?"

"It's private and personal, but it is regarding the deaths of his brothers. He will want to speak with me. Please get him my message and this number. Tell him I won't call again," said Alex before disconnecting the phone.

His next call was to Yutu. Alex hoped that he had been able to get Josh released and Josh and his family out of Koto's reach.

"Uncle Alex!" answered his niece.

"Cassie, why are you answering Yutu's phone? Did he tell you he could?"

"He didn't tell me I couldn't, and I recognized your number."

Logical, especially for a six-year-old. His brother's eldest daughter was smart and precocious. Alex only hoped that one day she, and her sister, would fall for a member of their clan and be turned to become one of them.

"I'm glad you only answered because you knew it was me, but you shouldn't answer other people's phones. But I'm glad I get to talk to you. Is your dad there with the rest of you?"

"Yep. Yutu picked up Mommy, Lesley, and me and then we went and got Daddy out of the hospital. Mommy says if it wasn't for you, Daddy could have died. Uncle Alex?"

"Yes, Cass?"

"Are you going to get the man who hurt Daddy? Lesley is scared he may come after us, but I told her we were safe with Yutu and Daddy."

"You tell Lesley that your Daddy and Yutu will keep you safe while I go make sure that anyone who wants to hurt our family knows they would answer to me."

She giggled. "Mommy said the same thing and said nobody messes with Uncle Alex."

"Your mommy is a smart girl."

"Yep. Daddy says that's why she married him instead of you."

Alex laughed out loud. He could just imagine Josh saying that.

"Uncle Alex, I heard Daddy telling Mommy that you were getting married. She didn't seem happy. Doesn't she like your girlfriend?"

Trying to explain the dynamics of Kodiak-shifter relationships to a six-year-old was not something he wanted to take on. He'd leave that to Josh and Allie down the road. "Your dad is right, and your mom hasn't met Flynn yet."

"Her name is Flynn? That's a funny name for a girl."

Alex chuckled. "It is. Her name is Flynn Montgomery and she teaches at a university like your daddy. But I think you'll like her. Is your daddy available?"

"He's taking a nap. Mommy's here though."

Alex heard the phone being handed to Allie.

"How's he feeling?" Alex asked his brother's mate.

"Recovering rapidly. I always forget how much more quickly you Kodiaks heal. What are you planning to do?"

"I've placed a call to David Koto. I'll see if I can broker a peace, but if not, I'll deal with him."

"I suppose I should admonish you not to hurt him, but if this bastard is a threat to my husband and my children, you need to kill him."

"Spoken like the mate to a Kodiak. Koto will either retreat or die. He is a threat to my Flynn as well."

"You do know I'm not happy about that situation…"

"I didn't imagine you would be, but it's our way Allie. Flynn is my mate. We will be bonded, and she will submit to me."

"Alex…"

"Enough, Allie. That Josh indulges you is Josh's choice, but as clan leader, I will not brook your interference in the traditions of our kind. Besides, Flynn will be happy. I will see to that. I'll keep in touch. Take care of Josh and the girls and try not to be too big a pain in the ass to Yutu."

He disconnected before Allie had a chance to subject him once again to a tirade. She was Josh's mate and made his brother happy; that made her his family and subject to his protection.

Deciding to give Koto a bit more time to return his call, Alex headed for his cabin. He wanted to ensure it was secure and that no trace of Flynn could be found.

Ah, Flynn, the very thought of her made him smile. Alex was not foolish enough to think that it would be smooth sailing from here on out. In fact, he was fairly sure they would lock horns on a regular basis. He supposed he shouldn't be looking forward to their confrontations, but he was. Forcing Flynn to yield to his authority had a definite appeal. He had no doubt as to who would be the victor in their contests and her surrender would be all the sweeter for it.

Her brother was someone Alex felt could be trusted with the secret of the Kodiak-shifters. Whether or not Flynn chose to share with him that she was no longer human was a choice he would leave to her. Whether or not she was to become a shifter was not.

• • • • • • •

Flynn had watched him leave and remained on the bed until she was sure he was gone. Then, she began a systematic search of the room. First, she visually scanned the room, then she began feeling all of the walls… every nook and cranny—looking for something out of place, some way of revealing a hidden exit.

She tried not to think about him but failed. Every time he crossed her mind, she could almost feel his touch, just as she had each time during the past two years; only now she had more memories to add to her reverie. Why did he have the ability to touch her in a way no other ever had? It wasn't just his sexual prowess, although that seemed to know no bounds, and it certainly wasn't his use of gentle caresses and honeyed words—there had been none. But there was something honest and true in his visceral possession of her body… something that spoke to some deep, dark part of her calling forth a response that she had never felt with anyone else.

Was that enough to base a life on? What was she thinking? She wanted no part of whatever it was he was offering in whatever demented fairytale she had stumbled into.

Her nipples beaded and her pussy pulsed in denial of her thoughts. It was as if he were some foreign substance and she was an addict. The last rational part of her brain told her to run, but the greater part of her being whispered for her to stay and assured her that safety as well as a life and love worth sacrificing everything for lay with the man who was also a beast.

Flynn had all but given up when her fingers found a small crevice in the rock that felt chiseled out by man and not made by mother nature. She probed it with her fingers looking to find how it worked or what it revealed. Finding nothing, she pressed and was surprised when the stone fireplace across the room clicked open. She crossed over to it and found that the stone fireplace and chimney was all one unit. It wasn't, as one would assume, affixed to the cavern wall, but rather to a unit designed to move.

She pushed on it and could smell fresh air and feel the cool air from the outside. Quickly she returned to the clothing he had left her and got dressed. He had provided everything she would need, not all of it intentionally. Gathering together some food, a gun, ammo, flares, and outerwear, she ventured into the corridor and pulled the escape hatch closed behind her until she heard it click back into place. Lighting one of the flares, she made her way towards freedom.

The passageway was dark, and the torch provided only the most minimal of light, but she made steady progress. The further she went, the fresher the air. After about what she estimated was no more than a half hour, she could see the proverbial light at the end of the tunnel. Once outside, she extinguished the flare, trying to get her bearings. Even though it was late spring, there was still some snow on Shuyak, especially on the higher areas of the island. The going was slippery, but she made steady progress. Thankfully, at this time of the year, there was almost perpetual daylight.

She figured they had entered the cavern to her right. That meant the best way to leave was down the hillside and to the left. She tried to recall from what direction they had come. Flynn was fairly sure that it too lay to the right, but decided to head up and to the left, before turning to go downhill. She needed to find running water and try to follow it back to the coastline. From there, she could figure out how to get to the ranger station.

She had no sooner begun her trek when it occurred to her that Alex was a ranger. She wondered if all of the rangers were some kind of shifter. Even if only those on Shuyak were, there would be no help for her there. Still, the ranger station should have kayaks or other ways of leaving the island. She formulated a plan to steal or borrow some means of escape and make use of it.

The going was rough, but Flynn was experienced and comfortable in the wilderness. She knew she needed to get out of the open. Without the ability to blend into the wooded areas or at least the tree line she would be far too easy to see. She had no doubt that if he spotted her, Alex would come for her. And if he used his ability to become a bear he could easily overtake and overpower her.

Her body seemed intent on betraying her. She was quite sure that if he caught her, he would spank her again and then fuck her with even more intensity and fervor than he had in the past. If he was truly a Kodiak, this was their mating season. If he shared those traits, and all indications were that he did, he would be in the grip of the need to rut, and as he saw her as his mate, he'd be looking to do so with her.

Why did the thought arouse and not disgust her? Each time he had fucked her had been more intensely satisfying than the last. Even when he was driving into her with a ferocity she had never experienced with anyone other than Alex, she felt more alive, more one with him than with anyone before. She had tried several times to have sex with a man after Alex but had been unable to do so. At some point she either realized she felt nothing, or the idea of another man touching her intimately was something she simply could not abide. So, for the past two years she had made do with pleasuring herself, which was far from satisfying. She grinned; she'd certainly made up for it in the past few days. Each time they had been together, he had ensured she had multiple orgasms before forcing her to come with him as he released what felt like a torrent of cum into her.

And what did he mean by being turned? Was it possible to become what he was? What would that be like to be able to shift fluidly from one form to another? And why did the idea not fill her with disgust and terror? She had convinced herself that she was not meant to be with a man in any kind of long-term, committed relationship—whether it be marriage or not. Was Alex right? Was she his mate? Was he her future? Would exploring a relationship with him be so bad? Would she be able to retain her own identity or would that be subjugated to his will along with her body?

Flynn shook her head to rid herself of such musings. She needed time and distance to figure out if she wanted any part of Alex Kingston... well, any part other than his cock as it stroked her pussy repeatedly until she had cried out his name in need and then fulfillment. That she already knew she wanted desperately.

She spied the tree line at the top of the ridge and picked up her pace. Until she made up her mind about how she felt, if anything, about Alex, she needed to keep moving and stay out of his hands. It was becoming obvious that each time he possessed her, she craved his touch that much more. What was worse was that she was fairly certain he knew it.

Once within the relative safety of the woods, she allowed herself a moment to catch her breath and take a long swallow of the cold water in her canteen. A canteen—who the hell used canteens anymore? She grinned. Apparently Kodiak bear shifters.

• • • • • • •

Koto had yet to call and even though Alex's cabin would

be difficult to find, he approached it with caution. After ensuring he was alone, Alex circled the cabin looking for any obvious signs that anyone had breached his security. Seeing none, he started to open the door. His excellent sense of hearing detected a click with just enough warning that he was able to fling himself off the porch. Rolling close to it, he saw the shrapnel and what had once been the front door blast past him. Koto had been there and left him a not very subtle message as to his intentions.

He stood and surveyed the damage as he grabbed the fire extinguisher out of his storage shed and put the fire out. He examined the explosive device. It had been shaped to focus its fury at whoever tripped it as they entered the cabin. Incongruously, the majority of the cabin looked untouched. He realized it wouldn't take much to restore the cabin to good working order. He ran his fingers through the residue and held them up to his nose. While he could still detect the faint, distinctive fragrance of his mate, he could also discern motor oil, the signature of the explosive C-4.

Alex began cleaning up the mess. He would need to board up the doorway, not only to keep out any animals who might think to take up residence while he was away, but to secure its contents. He was just nailing the last board into place when the sat phone rang. He glanced at the number… a Seattle area code.

"Koto," he answered.

"You are still alive. That's a pity, although I suppose a Kodiak with your skills will prove to be an interesting quarry."

"I think you're mistaken as to who is predator and who is prey. So far, it's Kodiak two, Komodo zero. You want to take a run at me, we can make it three/zip."

"And are you so certain of the outcome?"

"Given what's happened so far, I'm liking my odds a lot better than yours."

"But what of the woman?"

Alex had to suppress the growl that threatened to erupt

from his throat. Koto had said *the* woman, not *his* woman. That shouldn't be surprising, Komodos tended to have one female to several males; there were no strong emotional ties. Each male would breed the female during the mating season. Neither gender had any interest in sex outside the breeding season, which probably accounted for the Koto brothers' success, their focus had been on business not on the continuation of their line. It was said that female Komodos were capable of asexual reproduction, which Alex believed given how ugly the large lizards were.

Koto not knowing yet of his connection to Flynn was a good thing. If he did, her value as a target for his vengeance would skyrocket. As Alex knew the mating habits of Komodos, he was quite certain that Koto knew that Kodiak-shifters mated for life and were incredibly sexual, especially during their breeding season. The fact that Koto was keeping him from breeding his mate did nothing to foster any kind of warm, fuzzy feelings towards him.

"What of her?"

"I am not ignorant of who or what you are, Kingston. I would imagine that killing the Alpha of the Unangan Clan would ensure that your brother would lead your people in a holy war of sorts against me. That would be time consuming and not profitable. I would propose you turn the human female over to me, and we will be done with this unpleasantness between us."

"Unpleasantness? Is that what you call it? I kill two of your brothers…" started Alex.

"Leaving me to rule our empire alone and ensure that our female's eggs are fertilized only by me."

"That's cold even for a Komodo. If she is bound to you and you were to die, would any eggs that hatch inherit your fortune? Because I rather imagine she'd much prefer to reproduce without ever having to endure your breeding her."

Koto hissed. "You will not give up the woman? Why is that, I wonder? Has the Chief of the Unangan Clan taken her to mate? Interesting. And this is your breeding season as well. I suspect you would much rather be in the throes of the rut with your new female. What about her brother?"

Alex barked a laugh. "I'd always heard Komodos were fierce, but it seems you'd rather negotiate than fight."

"Why risk myself if we can find a mutually beneficial solution."

"Would those in your clutch see you as your brother's successor if they knew you were unwilling to avenge your brother?"

"Vengeance or justice can be had in many ways among my people. Ritual torture of the one responsible is valued in the same way as combat. And it could be argued that the brother is just as much at fault as you or the female. After all, he was the one Henry contracted with."

"That's a bit of a reach. After all, I'm the one who almost ripped Henry's head from his body and crushed Kevin's skull in the stream. Let me tell you plainly, I will fight you one-on-one and let that be the end of it. After all, your idiot brother brought this down on his head when he lied to Ben and Flynn and tried to kill a Kodiak, without a tag I might add. That's a violation of federal law. He only compounded his stupidity when he tried to kill my brother. At that point he put himself in my cross hairs."

"So, you have no argument with me personally… except for any damage done to your cabin, which I would be happy to pay for."

"Your brothers were fools, but I'm not. In order to save face, you have to avenge their deaths in some way. If you don't, I understand those in your clutch would replace you and that is a bloody and violent process."

"You are well educated about my kind," said Koto thoughtfully.

"Wasn't it Sun Tzu who said 'know your enemy'?"

"A Kodiak that thinks and not just reacts, an admirable adversary. So, you will not give either of the Montgomerys up?"

"My mate or her brother? Hardly. And make a play for them, for my brother or his family or anyone else under my protection, and no band of security men or assassins will stop me from ripping your throat out and making a pair of boots out of your scaly hide."

"So, we are at an impasse…"

"No, Koto, you and I are at war unless you choose to settle this with single combat."

"We both know I would lose in any contest with you. And you are right, my clutch will kill me if I do not show them I have avenged my brothers' deaths."

"You better come for me soon. I have already let it be known in Seattle's shifter community that your brothers died by my hand. Your options are limited. Fight me and die, or give up your empire and crawl back beneath whatever rock you slithered out from under."

Alex disconnected. It had occurred to him as he talked to Koto that there really was only one way for this to end… Koto either retreated to some sunny island where his clutch might not be bothered to come after him or he fought Alex and most likely died. He didn't envy the lizard's choices.

CHAPTER TEN

Flynn made the relative safety of the trees. She continued up the incline, hoping that at the top of the ridge she would be able to get an idea about where she was and how best to proceed. Once she got to the top, she ventured out from the woods and scanned the horizon. She could see the ocean and what she believed to be the remains of Port William. Once a thriving community, it had become a virtual ghost town used only as a destination to ferry tourists. There wouldn't be any help there, but it was at the southernmost tip of the island across a narrow strait of water. It might be possible to flag down a boat to get away.

She made her way down what most might call a mountain, but in the Pacific Northwest and Alaska was merely a large hill. The footing was loose and therefore precarious, but her boots offered good support and tread. She had almost reached the outskirts of the town when she heard a heavy crunch behind her. Flynn whirled around expecting to see Alex in either his bear or human form… When had thinking of him that way become normal? Instead, what she saw were two large monitor lizards. The Komodos had called in reinforcements.

The phone call with Koto had left Alex in an oddly exhilarated mood. There was a part of him that felt he should be apprehensive and on edge. After all, he had basically declared war on Koto and his clutch of Komodos. But the idea of a physical battle and protecting his mate filled him with a sense of purpose and lust. He smiled. Any thoughts that even touched on Flynn brought forth a new surge of arousal. He needed to end this fight with Koto so that he could fully engage in the battle to bring Flynn into the clan.

His comment to her before he left, that he planned to fuck her again upon his return had not been idle. She had best get used to the fact that he was not often subtle or romantic and that she would serve his more-than-healthy libido. Flynn might make a token protest or snarl at him afterwards, but he had yet to plunge his cock to the depths of her cunt and not find it warm, wet, and alive with sensation. His mate was wildly responsive and had a deep well of passion he intended to explore more fully. For now, he almost hoped she wouldn't be waiting and there would be some sign she had tried to escape. He found that spanking Flynn served as excellent foreplay for them both.

Alex was skirting the outer rim of the ridge that held his den when he spied footprints—ones too small to be made by a man and most definitely human. Flynn. He broke into a run and headed for the hidden escape tunnel from the cavern. There was the proof of her cleverness. Somehow, Flynn had found the secret emergency exit and managed to open it and use it. Once again, she had left him and was headed into a danger she couldn't possibly comprehend. When he caught up to her, not only would she understand the danger from Koto, but she would be fully cognizant of the consequences of defying him.

He realized as he tracked her that she hadn't bothered to try and hide her tracks. Knowing he could make better time in his bear form, Alex undressed, gathered his clothing, boots, and weapon, and called forth his bear self. Picking up the bundle, he began racing after her. He couldn't help but be proud of her. Instead of heading straight down the side of the cliff, she had gone up and away from the direction they'd come. She was finding a vantage point. Unfortunately for Flynn, he knew where she'd most likely head… Port William.

Alex loped along the side of the hill until he intersected with her footprints. That was all well and good until he found the second and third sets of tracks that were following hers. He picked up the pace and raced towards Port William. It was mostly likely deserted at this time of year so a perfect place for Koto's people to exact revenge on him and Flynn. If they harmed so much as one hair on her head, he would kill them, dispose of their bodies, and exact a terrible revenge on Koto and his entire clutch. If Flynn managed to keep herself safe, he would find a place to stash them and then determine how to exact the maximum leverage from their failure… and Flynn would learn the consequences for defying her mate.

The scent wafting up from the tracks told him that two Komodo dragons were trailing Flynn. She was still ahead of them, but he doubted that she had any idea that she was in danger. He increased his speed.

∙ ∙ ∙ ∙ ∙ ∙ ∙

The two lizards realized they now had their prey in sight and that she knew they were there. Unlike Alex, they were far quicker and more nimble in their human form. The larger of the two wriggled out of the bundle he had carried. The air around them seemed to shimmer and the two Komodos became large, well-muscled, naked men. Unwrapping the bundle, they each withdrew a handgun with a silencer.

Flynn headed for one of the abandoned warehouses

down by the docks. She needed to find a place where she could set herself up to take her best shot. She had used guns before and was a decent shot. She remembered once hearing that if you were trying to ensure whoever you shot at would be incapable of coming after you to aim for dead center mass. That way if you weren't an expert, the chances are you would still hit something.

She could hear them running behind her, gaining ground with each stride. She spotted an opening in the wall of one of the warehouses. The idea of being trapped inside flitted across her mind, but the ability to hide and find a secure location from which to shoot outweighed the uncertain safety of open ground. She slipped through the opening and spied a likely set of boxes that would offer her some protection as well as a place to brace her rifle.

Later, she would swear she never heard a gunshot. She felt a hot, stabbing pain in her chest as blood burst through her sweater. It was as if her body was operating on an engine and someone flipped the off switch. Her arms flew up, the rifle flying out of her grasp as her legs carried her one… two… three steps and she collapsed. The last thing she heard before the darkness descended was the roar of an angry Kodiak bear… Alex most likely. The thought passed through the last of her consciousness to be grateful that he had come after her and would avenge her death and how sad it was that she hadn't had the courage to explore what might have been between them.

· · · · · · ·

Alex saw Flynn dash into the warehouse followed closely by the two Komodos. He heard the report of a silenced weapon and saw Flynn fall as he burst through an exterior window into the dark, cavernous space, lit by dirty windows that only allowed minimal light through the grimy windows. His eyes adjusted quickly to the darkness as he charged her assailants, roaring in anger, fear, and grief. The two assassins sent by Koto barely had time to process that there had been a sound, much less the threat that sound represented. Alex body slammed into the one closest to him, knocking him out of the way.

He rounded on the first man as he rolled away and shifted into a Komodo dragon. The beast lumbered towards him, its massive jaws snapping, trying to sink its serrated teeth into any one of Alex's limbs. Alex swung his massive paw, catching the creature under its jaw, slamming its jaw shut and flipping it up and away from where it could harm either him or Flynn.

He turned back to the first man as he shook his head, getting to his feet. Alex shifted back to his human form, grasped the man by either side of his head and twisted, snapping his neck cleanly. He heard the second assassin trying to make a run for it. Glancing at Flynn and seeing the red stain spreading across her chest, he shifted and rushed after the man who had brought her down. Flynn's remaining assailant hadn't made the door when Alex caught him, spinning him around before slashing his jugular with his razor-sharp claws and watching the man's blood bubble as he gurgled and the light fled from his eyes.

Shifting back, he ran to Flynn, dropping and sliding on his knees so that he could cradle her in his arms.

"Oh, God, Flynn..." he cried, lifting her as gently as he could so that her upper body was leaning against his thighs.

The blood continued to seep out of the wound in her chest. It was no longer gushing, but he could see its proximity to her heart influencing the rhythm with which it pumped. Her eyes flickered open and he thought he saw the ghost of a smile cross her lips. She raised her hand weakly and touched his cheek in a gesture of acceptance and farewell. If she thought she would escape her destiny with him by dying, she had best have another thought.

Alex jerked his hunting knife from its sheath and sliced open one of his veins on the underside of his wrist. Quickly he pressed the gash to her injury, forcing his own life's blood into her and willing her to live. He watched as her eyes shuttered closed and her body trembled as it tried to find peace in death. He could feel her life slipping away.

"Don't die, Flynn. Live!" he whispered. Had he been too late? Had the damage to her frail human system been too great?

He continued to press the underside of his forearm to her open wound. A wave of dizziness passed through him, but he shook it off, refusing to remove the only chance she had at not succumbing to death's siren song. If he could infuse enough of his blood with hers, he could initiate the change. That would, in theory, force some of the internal damage done by the would-be assassin's bullet to begin to heal itself. There were written accounts of humans being turned when they were near death. Some had survived; some had not. Alex willed Flynn to be one of the former.

Normally, the turning of one's mate was done at their bonding ceremony. The couple would each make a deep, ritualized cut in the palm of their hand. The hands would then be bound together with a special sash. The benefits of the change, if successful, were almost instantaneous. Whether or not the transition would result in the recipient surviving and being turned could take a few days to several weeks. During that time, the beneficiary of the gift was cared for generally by the one who had initiated the change or that Kodiak's family and friends. If the recipient's body rejected becoming a shifter, it was almost always swift and usually fatal.

Alex rocked back, his heart constricting in guilt and grief. What had he done? His actions had set in motion the events that had brought them here. Granted, he had done what he had to save his brother and then Flynn, but he had failed to kill the remaining Koto brother and now he had exacted his revenge. His actions had been instrumental in bringing about her death. The pain caused him to keen in a mournful sound that filled and reverberated throughout the abandoned building. He could feel her life slipping away and vowed to destroy Koto and his entire clutch.

He couldn't tear his eyes from her and watched as her breathing became more shallow and irregular. He knew she was near the end and he leaned down, kissing her gently.

"I love you, my mate; your death will not go unavenged and our people will mourn your passing."

He couldn't take his eyes from her face. If she opened her eyes again, he wanted her to know she wasn't alone and that a part of his spirit would accompany her into the afterlife. He would sing her death song.

"Great Spirit, my mate, the other half of my soul waits on death's doorstep. I would ask that you return her to me, but if you cannot do so, then take her and welcome her at your council fire. She is wild and untried in the ways of our people, but she carries my blood and embodies those things that are at the core of our being—courage, strength, and honor."

Alex sat holding her, praying that she was not in pain or afraid. He couldn't take his eyes off the slow rise and fall of her chest as she breathed. Little by little, her breathing evened out and the blood that had once seeped unobstructed from her chest, slowed to a trickle, and then stopped. Fearing the worst, Alex placed his ear to her chest; her heartbeat was weak but growing steady. Setting her down carefully, he left her momentarily to retrieve the sat phone.

"King?" came Yutu's voice over the line.

"Yutu, I need a medic and one of the seaplanes at the old warehouse in Port William."

"What are you doing there?"

He smiled as he cradled Flynn in his arms.

"Witnessing a miracle."

"What?" asked the normally stoic Yutu incredulously.

"Unless I am sadly mistaken, I am watching my mate claw her way back from the brink of death. She should be dead… they put a hole in her chest."

"Wouldn't it be better to have the hospital send a life flight?"

"She is beyond their help and capability. Koto's assassins shot her. The bullet should have killed her. I couldn't just watch her die without doing something."

The air hung heavy between them with silence.

"You turned her, didn't you?" Yutu whispered.

"I had no choice."

"There is always a choice and it was not yours to make," he admonished.

"She was incapable of making it. Regardless, I would have turned her when we took our vows."

Alex could hear movement on the other end of the phone.

"Alex?" asked Josh.

"Does Yutu have our people en route?" demanded Alex.

He was alpha to the clan; his word was law and would be accepted and obeyed unless someone wanted to challenge him for leadership.

"Yes. Of course, but Alex…"

"There is no but, Josh. She is my mate. She was dying and I did what was necessary to save her. She can have the rest of our lives to rail at me for that decision, but she, like the rest of you, will have to accept that. If someone wants to dispute my right to make that decision…"

"Don't be an ass. No one is going to challenge you. You are too well liked and respected. The Clan has thrived under your rule. I'm just saying that there may be some who question whether or not you had the right to make that decision."

"Your Allie among them?" asked Alex.

"Not if you lead with you've been head over heels in love with her for more than two years and she was dying. She's a bit of a romantic, my Allie."

"She is my mate. She is subject to my rule and I did what I had to in order to save her so she could bear our offspring."

"Trust me, the head over heels thing is the way to go… especially with your Flynn. She may not be all that thrilled about you having usurped her humanity."

"If that's the only thing…"

"Only thing?"

"Only thing she objects to, I will count myself most fortunate. I rather suspect it will be the least of the things she takes issue with. Besides, if I hadn't replaced some of her blood with mine, she wouldn't have survived. The internal damage is already repairing itself but she's going to need time to recover… before I beat her pretty ass for almost getting herself killed."

Josh laughed. "And they say romance is dead. Yutu says the plane should be there in thirty to forty minutes. Are you planning to bring her back here?"

"Yes, away from prying eyes. My mate is a woman of strong passions, which often lead her to make foolish decisions. She will need to learn that she is subject to my authority and that when she misbehaves or endangers herself that she will pay the price for her actions."

"I would think having her humanity stolen without any say-so is more than enough."

"Perhaps, but she was going to become Kodiak…"

"Because you said so?" Josh laughed again. "Let me know how that works for you. Wait, Yutu wants to speak to you."

"My Chieftain, your lodge is being prepared," the elder member of the clan said in a flat, but respectful tone.

"You don't approve."

"Your actions do not require my approval or consent."

"I am aware of that, but nonetheless, you don't. Your Lena isn't shifter born…"

"And gave her consent freely. She is a handful on the best of days. I'm not questioning what you did. In those circumstances I would have done the same. I'm just saying you might want to come at the whole, 'oh by the way, you're no longer human' thing in a little less dictatorial manner than you are inclined to do. From what Josh has shared, your Flynn makes my Lena look like the sweetest, most malleable of mates."

Alex chuckled softly. Referring to Lena as a handful was a gross understatement. He had shared many a campfire with Yutu when Lena needed something soft to sit on.

"But the best mates are always those with the most spirit. And even those females born Kodiak do not always take to being bonded and mated."

It was Yutu's turn to laugh. "That is true. Perhaps when your mate is through the change, your battles with her can provide the entertainment and supplant the stories of mine with Lena."

"Gods, I hope not. Did she really once hoist you off the ground by a fishing hook?"

"She did."

"That had to hurt," quipped Alex.

"Not nearly as much as her backside after I got down and put her over my knee." The smile in Yutu's voice was easy to hear. "May you be as blessed in your choice of mate as I have been in mine."

"Yutu, let everyone know they need to be vigilant. Koto sent two goons to get Flynn. He can't back off; his clutch would kill him."

"What will you do?"

"Once I am sure Flynn is safely through the change, I will leave her with our people while I deal with Koto."

"We'll see you when you arrive. Simon happened to be here in the village and is on the plane. Your mate will be in good hands." Simon was the clan's doctor as had been his father before him.

"Good. I'm going to take care of these two bodies."

"Do you think this may be the start of a war between our clan and Koto's clutch?"

"I'm hopeful that I can keep that from happening…"

"We will fight with you, my Chieftain."

"I know you would, but I think if I send pictures of the dead bodies along with how this came about to the Komodo ruling tribunal, I can box him in. I challenged him to single combat, and he refused. I'm hopeful that the Komodos as a whole, and perhaps even his clutch will force him to clean up his brother's mess on his own."

"Regardless of their decision, they will not win. We will destroy them if we have to. I'll see you when you get here. Just try to stay out of Simon's way."

"What do you mean by that?"

"You forget, I had to watch Lena make the transition. I would rather face a thousand Komodos on my own than do that again. Simon had to threaten to shoot me with a tranquilizer dart before I'd let him do what he needed to help her," Yutu said laughing.

"I'll try, but I'm not promising anything. I'm afraid my emotions run hot where Flynn is concerned."

"If they didn't, she wouldn't be your mate."

"True enough. I'll see you soon. And thanks for getting Josh and his family out of harm's way."

"It was easy enough to do. Allie is being the perfect model of a mate and the two girls seem to be enjoying themselves. I will not be surprised if the older one does not choose to embrace her Kodiak heritage," remarked Yutu.

"Me either. But don't say anything to Allie. She'd have a conniption fit and Josh needs to focus on healing."

"I would never have said anything, but it was Allie who made the remark to me."

"Huh. Who'd have thought?" Alex said before disconnecting.

Once again, Alex lowered Flynn to the ground, gratified to see the loss of blood had stopped. He made a pillow for her head out of his jacket and then used his phone to take pictures of the two dead men before wrapping each in old canvas and rope he found in the warehouse. If Simon said that Flynn was stable enough, he'd have the plane take them out over deep water and toss them into the sea. If she wasn't, he'd wait until they got to the village and bury them.

Hearing the seaplane land on the water, he ran to the ocean-side door to the warehouse and opened it. Simon rushed in, medical bag in hand, and hurried to where Alex pointed, while Alex helped the pilot load the bodies into the back. Once that was done, he joined the doctor who was attending Flynn.

"They weren't kidding around when they shot her," Simon said.

"I know. How is she? What are her chances?"

"I think I'd be lying if I said they were even as good as fifty/fifty. She had to be pretty weak when you got your blood into her. Let me take a look at your arm," he said reaching for Alex's arm.

"My arm is fine. See to my mate."

"Once I get her back to the compound, I can give her supportive care, but her body is either going to accept the gift or not. I will tell you this, it has already stopped the damage and begun to repair it. For what it's worth, if you hadn't done what you did, she would be dead. There's no doubt in my mind about that. The rest," he said, indicating Flynn's trembling body, "is up to her."

Alex lifted Flynn in his strong arms and accompanied Simon back to the plane. They strapped her onto a makeshift gurney as the plane taxied along the surface of the water before gracefully lifting off. They made a wide swing over deep water and when neither radar or scanning the area with binoculars revealed anything, Simon and Alex heaved the bodies over the side. Thirty minutes later they landed and floated up to the seaplane's dock where several members of the clan waited with a proper litter to take Flynn to Alex's family lodge.

"She'll be all right there?" he asked Simon.

"Not much that I can do to help her except through IV immune suppressants, vitamins, fluids, and the like. I thought both of you would be more comfortable up at your place. I can take her to the clinic if you like…"

"No, you're right. She'll be more comfortable in our bed, and hers is the only comfort that counts."

Simon laid his hand on Alex's forearm. "I will say this

again; she would be dead if you hadn't given her your blood. That gunshot should have killed her. The fact that it didn't is testament to her strength. And she made it through the plane ride with very little change in her vitals. Your mate is strong and wants to live. Have faith in her."

Alex accompanied them to the lodge where he was intercepted by his two nieces.

"Why don't you stay down here for a few minutes while we get Flynn all set up? I'll let you know when you can come up," said Simon.

Alex nodded.

"Uncle Alex, is that your mate?" asked Cassie.

"Is she going to be all right?" asked Lesley.

Alex smiled. He adored his brother's children. "Yes, and yes. As soon as the doctor says it's all right, I'll take you up to meet her and you can help me look after her. Would you like that?"

Both little girls nodded and then giving their uncle a hug ran back outside to join the other children of the village.

"I forget how much they love it up here," said Allie before taking his hand in hers and squeezing it reassuringly.

"She'll be fine," said Josh, joining them. "She's tough. She has no choice if she's to be mated to you."

"Does she know you're planning to make her your mate?" asked Allie, trying to keep her tone neutral.

"Allie, don't start. Alex has enough on his mind."

"Let her get it out of her system, Josh. I have told Flynn she is my mate and I turned her without asking her."

"As she was on the brink of death, I'm willing to give you a pass on that one," teased Allie.

Alex leaned down and kissed her cheek, "How very generous of you," he replied, smiling. "I know you don't always understand or agree with our ways, but I'm going to ask that you refrain from encouraging Flynn to do anything stupid. The stakes are too high right now."

"So, you're all right if I support dangerous behavior after you defeat Koto?" she quipped.

Alex chuckled. "Sure, as long as you're fine with me ordering my brother to beat your ass. Are you so sure I'll win?"

"There are two things I've always known about you, Alex. The first is I've never known anyone who could best you if it was important."

"And the second?" he asked genuinely interested.

"That you're a chauvinistic, arrogant sonofabitch."

"Allie," growled Josh at his wife.

Alex laughed. "Don't fuss at her when she's right, baby brother. And you were right earlier when you said Flynn would have to be tough to be mated to me." With that, he turned and trotted up the stairs.

"You aren't really annoyed at me, are you?" he heard Allie ask Josh.

"No, I think it helped."

It was then he heard something he'd never thought he would, the sharp thwack as Josh's hand connected with his mate's backside… and her responding giggle. Out of sight, he leaned against the wall and took a deep breath. If Flynn was awake, he didn't want her to see any weakness in him.

CHAPTER ELEVEN

The next week was absolute torture. Watching Flynn's body going through a transition it was too weak to actually survive was the worst thing he'd ever been through. There was nothing he could do to help her. Simon reassured him over and over that each day Flynn didn't die, her chances improved.

The day after he had brought Flynn to the compound, he worked with Yutu to craft a message to be delivered to the Komodo's ruling tribunal. Yutu, the clan's consigliere, for lack of a better term, carried the message himself and was due back today.

"Alex?" said Allie sticking her head in their room. "Yutu is back. Why don't you go downstairs and talk to him and take a break? I know, I know, you don't need a break. But you do. Lena knew he was coming and is downstairs making something to eat. Grab a shower and go down and join them. I'll stay here with Flynn and tell her all the rotten things she and I can do when she's well."

He smiled. He had always liked Allie, but until now he had doubted that his brother was the dominant partner in their relationship. He had no such concerns now and had come to respect their partnership. Allie had been an inordinate amount of help and he was grateful.

"Thanks, Allie. I can't thank you enough…"

"Then don't even bother to try. That's what families are for. Now shoo!"

Alex stood under the pulsing shower and let its hot water do what it could for the knotted muscles in his neck, shoulders, and back. Once he was clean, he dressed in jeans and a flannel shirt, not bothering with socks or shoes, and padded down the staircase.

"Yutu," he said, extending his hand.

"Alex…"

"Before you two get started, why don't you sit down and eat."

Alex kept himself from growling, but only barely.

"Lena is right," said Yutu. "And I bring good news; Koto is on his own."

Alex nodded as they all sat down. Josh's children joined them and so they kept the conversation light-hearted and sent them to help Lena in the kitchen when their lunch had been consumed.

"What did they say?" asked Alex.

"I got the distinct impression that the Kotos have never been overly popular with their governing body. They were more than a bit dismayed at what had taken place and wanted me to assure you that none of it had been sanctioned. They gave me their pledge that they would not interfere, except…"

"And they were doing so well. I will not allow them to give David Koto a slap on the wrist and call it a day."

"They don't expect you to. Your reputation preceded my visit. Apparently, you saved the life of one of their member's sons in a firefight. They were quick to point out, had they known, they would have stopped Henry from going hunting. It seems they felt what happened was predictable. They want no part of a war between the Komodos and the Kodiaks. They asked if you would be willing to restrict your vengeance to David Koto himself and let the clutch live.

They don't believe the others had anything to do with it and the men Koto used were mercenaries and outcasts from their society."

"In other words, they went belly up and threw Koto under the bus," said Josh.

Yutu nodded. "They did indeed. I told them I thought you would agree to their terms and if not, I would let them know within twenty-four hours of my returning home."

"If I agree…"

"I need do nothing and the matter is concluded as far as they are concerned."

"Then your work on this matter is finished," said Alex. "Once Flynn is out of danger, I will issue Koto a formal challenge. If he refuses, I will head to Seattle and hunt him down. I mean to rip that lizard's lungs out."

"There's a visual image I can't unsee," said Lena, returning. "If you are done, I'd like to take my mate home. It is the season, my mate had been gone for three days, and my sister is keeping our children until tomorrow morning."

The quiet, low growl from Yutu's throat was filled with lust and Alex waved him off.

"Thank you, Yutu, for all your help. Now, go see to your mate. I do believe she plans to have her way with you."

"It is I who will have my way with my naughty mate for being so bold in front of our clan leader."

Before she could do anything about it, Yutu had hoisted Lena over his shoulder and headed out of the Kingston lodge.

All alone, Josh looked at his brother. "If you'd rather, I can take care of Koto for you."

"No, Flynn is my mate."

"That makes her my family too. After all, Henry shooting me is what started this whole thing."

"You stay out of it. You can serve me best by continuing to heal and remaining up here to ensure Flynn and your family's safety."

"What about Flynn's brother?"

"I called him at a time he and I had pre-arranged."

"Then I'm surprised he isn't here."

"I persuaded him that it was better for Flynn and to our mutual advantage if he stayed put."

"I'm surprised he was willing to listen. Does he know about Flynn?"

"That she's been shot and is healing, yes. The rest of it, no. I want to talk to Flynn before we tell him."

"I don't envy you that conversation… with either of them."

"I will leave it up to Flynn as to how much she tells him about our kind."

"You aren't worried about him?"

Alex shook his head. "No. He's an honorable guy and loves his little sister. As long as I can keep her safe and happy, I don't think he'll much care."

"Good enough."

"I want to get back up to Flynn. I know that the compound is the most secure location for her to be in. But Josh, when I take on Koto, I need to know you'll keep her safe, regardless of what happens."

Josh looked his brother dead in the eye. "If she is your mate, she is my family. You're not the only Kingston that will do whatever it takes to keep his family from harm."

Alex nodded as he headed up the stairs. He entered the room to find Allie reading to Flynn.

"She seemed upset when you first left, but once I started reading to her, she settled. I think she seems better from when I last saw her," she said.

"I agree."

"What did Yutu have to say?"

"Other than he planned to make up for lost time with his mate?"

Allie snorted.

"As we thought, the Komodo tribunal knew nothing about what was going on and wanted no part of a war with us. They assured Yutu that Koto acted alone and have basically sanctioned my killing him."

Allie sighed. "There was a time I would have decried that kind of violence for any reason, but now that Koto has tried to kill people I care about, I want you to wipe his presence from this earth."

"That's my plan. Now, why don't you and Josh take the girls and go do something fun. The salmon are running and there are several fish ladders. They might enjoy seeing them jumping up out of the water."

"Would you mind if they came in to say good night to Flynn before they go to bed tonight?"

"I think that would be nice. Now, go spend some time with your family."

Allie stood on her tiptoes and brushed her lips against his cheek. "You and Flynn are my family too."

She squeezed his forearm reassuringly before leaving the room.

∙ ∙ ∙ ∙ ∙ ∙ ∙

Flynn had felt the searing pain moments before crumbling to the ground, blackness overtaking her. She recalled seeing Alex's stricken face; he'd looked frightened. She couldn't imagine anything that could scare him. There had been pain and then peace as it felt as though her spirit relinquished its connection with her body. Then the feel of being pressed back down into the earth and hearing a long, mournful cry. As it receded, darkness and calm overtook her again.

Curiously, on some level, Flynn knew she was dreaming. Two distinct dreams seemed to run in an endless loop, both involving being spanked and fucked by Alex. The first was a dream she was all too familiar with… the memory of their first time together in Seattle. But the second was no memory… was it a fantasy? Something she hoped would happen? A harbinger of the future?

She could feel Alex's anger with her and could hear his

angry tone, although the words were indistinct. She was naked. Flynn wondered why in all of her dreams with Alex she was always naked.

They were in her houseboat in Seattle—someplace Alex had never been. His fist tangled in her long hair and he dragged her from the door into the main lounge, sitting down on the sofa and tossing her over his hard, muscular thighs with the telltale outline of his bulging cock.

He brought his hand down on her ass with a resounding crack as it made impact. Alex spanked her with the same strength and tempo she had experienced more than once in real life. His hand covered the entire expanse of her rump in a systematic way, never landing a blow in the same spot twice, but somehow overlapping and compounding the heat and pain. She kicked her legs, trying to squirm away from him, but never seemed to get anywhere.

Over and over he swatted her backside with even more sting. As in real life, he didn't stop until she abandoned any kind of stoic response and began to wail and beg him to stop.

Once she reached the point where she didn't think she could take any more, he stood, unceremoniously dumping her on the floor, before fisting her hair again. He hauled her to her feet and then forced her over the end of the couch, pinning her in place while he stepped behind her. She heard his zipper being drawn down as he spread her legs, guiding his cock to tease her swollen labia before surging forward, completely engulfing himself in her warmth.

"Naughty mates get their bottoms spanked and their pussies fucked," he said as he pumped in and out, his groin making harsh contact with her punished ass.

So intense was her arousal, she could barely breathe as her inner walls shook and quivered. There was no way, even in her dream, to comprehend her primitive response to his treatment of her. The spanking ramped up her passion and he seemed intent on extracting as much pleasure from his use of her as he could. Flynn's breathing became shallower and in syncopated rhythm to his thrusting. She wondered where the soft mewling noises were coming from and realized they were coming from her. Alex's groaning was in perfect time and harmony to the sounds she was making.

Flynn started to pant as she neared the edge of completion. Sensing her impending climax, he plunged harder and deeper so that he pounded her pussy with feral abandon. He gave a last brutal thrust, and she toppled into the abyss of ecstasy, screaming his name. Her pussy spasmed as it contracted all along his length. She writhed in his hold as his cum gushed into her, bathing her wrecked inner walls, savoring her response. Her orgasmic tremors continued as his cock twitched inside her, dispersing the last of his seed and inflicting little mini-orgasms on her as she cried softly in complete and abject submission while he finished.

The dreams were wildly erotic and devastatingly humiliating. She would never admit to finding Alex's dominant possession of her body and soul both so arousing and comforting. There was a sense of satisfaction of a long-held, but unspoken need, to submit to him. Her body shuddered violently as it ascended from the inky depths of unconsciousness, determinedly seeking the light despite her desire to stay shrouded in the shadows.

"Flynn? Flynn?" she heard him say. "Josh? Allie? Somebody get Simon!" Alex bellowed.

"Jesus, Alex, could you keep it down?" she moaned. "I have the mother of all headaches. In fact, it only hurts slightly less than the rest of my body. I'd kind of gotten used to having a sore ass and pussy since you came charging into my life, but this is on a whole other level."

Alex crushed her to him, squeezing the breath from her lungs. "Flynn, you're alive."

"Well, duh. You're squishing me. I'm too weak to run. Could you… oh shit, Alex," she said, panicked as she glanced around what appeared to be a well-appointed bedroom. "There were two Komodos…"

"They can't hurt you; they're dead."

Flynn looked down; she was dressed in a delicate nightgown that appeared to be made out of gossamer silk. Her chest which should, she remembered, have a large hole in it, appeared to be completely healed.

Seeing the alarmed look in her eyes, he said, "You're fine; the damage from the gunshot…"

"I was shot?"

"Yes, but it has healed completely."

"How? Wait, are you hurt? I recall blood… so much blood," she whispered.

"I had a small, self-inflicted wound which is healed. Koto's assassins are dead."

"You killed them, right? I hope so. I probably should be upset that you killed them, but I'm not. We're going to have to kill David Koto…"

"*We* will do nothing of the sort. *I* will deal with Koto, but I agree that until he breathes his last, he will not stop."

Three people she didn't recognize burst through the door.

"Flynn, I see you decided to join us," said a man who appeared to be Alex's double.

"I'm Allie, Josh's wife," said a beautiful blonde, standing at the end of the bed and indicating Alex's twin brother. "And this is Simon. He's the doctor up here and has been taking care of you."

Alex pulled Flynn forward and plumped pillows behind her back before laying her back to rest against them. She found it odd that he knew how to plump pillows.

"Simon, take a look at her. How is she?" asked Alex.

The doctor sat on the edge of the bed, listened to her heart, and took her vital signs. "She appears to be completely healed…"

"How long have I been out of it?" asked Flynn.

"Several days," said Simon, looking at her over his glasses. "Why don't you tell me how you feel?"

"Like shit," snapped Flynn, "and like I told Alex, I have

the mother of all hangovers."

"Bad enough that you'd like me to give you something?" he asked solicitously.

"Just some aspirin or ibuprofen," she answered. "Where did all of you come from and where am I?"

Simon stood and turned to Alex. "She's come through the transition just fine. It seems to have resolved anything that might have resulted from the gunshot. I'd like her to take it easy for a few days, but then she should be as good as new… better even."

"What's he talking about?" snarled Flynn.

"Calm down, Flynn. No one here will hurt you," said Alex reassuringly.

"That's not technically true, bro," said Josh with smiling eyes. It was interesting, the two men appeared to be identical twins. But Josh's features seemed to be somehow softer—his eyes quick to gleam with amusement and his overall countenance lighter than Alex who had a tendency to glower. "Just last night you were saying how you couldn't wait until she was healed so you could… how did you put it? Oh yes, beat her ass until she never even thinks to try and escape you again," he continued, laughing as he finished.

"You're not helping, Josh," said Alex exasperatedly.

"You're right, he's not," said the pretty blonde, standing at the end of the bed. "Simon, do you think she's strong enough to take a shower? I imagine that would go a long way towards making her feel better."

"Yo, Allie, you might try addressing these remarks to me. I've had it with people telling me what to do," Flynn said, flinging back the covers.

"Flynn," growled Alex, "these people have been looking after you. Behave yourself."

Flynn swung her legs over the edge of the bed and tried to stand up, a wave of dizziness forcing her to sit back down. She batted at Alex's hand as he steadied her.

"Don't…" She felt herself swaying. "So much blood."

"It's all right, Flynn, you're safe now. No one here will hurt you."

Flynn pushed at him. "Leave me alone. I want a shower and to get dressed. Then I'm going home." She stood again, this time using the bedpost for support.

"Flynn, please let me help you," said Allie.

"You know, Flynn, that might not be a bad idea," offered Simon. "If you get lightheaded in the shower you could bang your head."

"If she isn't safe in the shower, I will take her," growled Alex.

"Doesn't anyone hear me? I'm fine. I'm taking a shower and I'm going home."

"You are home," said Alex with a sensual snarl as he pulled her into his arms.

Why had she never noticed before how incredibly sexy he was? Wait, that wasn't true, she'd noticed, oh God, how she'd noticed.

The very thought of him was enough to make her nipples bead and desire to swirl in her nether regions before invading her entire body. The idea of a shower with Alex Kingston had a certain appeal. Certainly, getting to feel his strong hands caressing her body, leaning against his muscular frame and feeling his cock, swollen between them had a great deal of appeal. In fact, the idea of fucking him sounded like a much better idea than just taking a shower.

She could feel the engorged bulge pulsing between them, behind the fly of his jeans. Flynn maneuvered her hand so that she was able to slip it between them and down past the inside of his waistband. Alex groaned as she gently fondled him. She was not expecting the harsh, staccato slap that landed on her behind. She tried to jump back but was held firmly in place.

"I told you to behave. If I have to tell you again, it will be more than one swat that lands on your backside." He turned to the doctor. "Just how recovered is she?"

Simon chuckled. "Recovered enough that you can deal

with your mate as you see fit within limits—nothing too harsh or strenuous."

"In other words, asshole, we could have fucked," hissed Flynn, feeling her nipples continuing to tighten as her pussy threatened to drip its need down the inside of her thigh.

"And we will," grumbled the beast who held her close and who she could feel was barely keeping his anger and lust in check. "The rest of you," he said over his shoulder, "get out."

"Alex…" started Allie.

"Allie, we talked about this. Stay out of it," said Josh, taking his wife by the hand. "We'll give the two of you a little privacy."

Once they were alone, Alex drew the nightgown over her head and gently lowered her back to the bed, following her down with his own body.

"I have missed you, mate. I thought I might have lost you," he murmured, parting her thighs with his knees and kissing her mouth, stopping to suckle her nipples before engulfing the entire areola surrounding them.

Without thought Flynn arched her back, pushing the entirety of her breast deeper into his mouth. She grasped his forearms and reveled in his sensual onslaught. Alex seemed unhurried and took time to ensure both nipples were fully engorged, and her arousal completely awakened.

"I… I," he started.

"Shh," she said, placing her hand over his mouth. "I don't want to talk, Alex, I just want to feel. I just want you."

He grinned at her before continuing to make his way down her body until he settled himself between her legs so that his mouth would now be able to pleasure her. His muscular arms wrapped around her thighs, parting the wet folds of her vulva. Lowering his head, he sucked the swollen nubbin at the apex of her thighs into his mouth, wrapping his tongue around it and sucking. Her hips undulated, spreading her legs and offering herself more fully to him. Her world spun out of control, pussy aching with emptiness, but throbbing. As he sucked the small button between her legs, Flynn felt her impending climax as it rushed towards her, threatening to tear her world apart.

Alex reached under her, his finger rimming and then entering the tight ring of muscle guarding her back passage. It gave way, allowing him to penetrate and stroke her there as his other hand pressed her into the mattress as he pinched and tugged on her nipples. She felt an orgasm crashing down upon her and cried out. He allowed her to experience its full power until the tremors ceased and he returned to sucking and nibbling on her again. Now when she squirmed, it was not to get away from him.

Flynn's second climax was faster and more intense, enveloping her in a haze of feeling centered solely on his mouth and what he was doing. She vaguely remembered that at some point before this she'd wanted to get away from him, but all she could do was press her mons more fully into his face so that his licking, nipping, and sucking had greater impact on her desire. Alex nuzzled her clit and kissed it before turning his attention to her molten core, dripping from its desire for his possession. He plunged his tongue into her, tasting her sweet elixir as she pushed herself against his face. Lapping up her honey, he encouraged her to produce more for his use. He thrust his tongue up into her and swirled it around making her cry out. The walls of her sheath clamped down, pulsating with a deep and old rhythm.

She clutched at his head as his hands slid under her body and he placed each of her legs over his shoulder on either side of his head. This was a new assault on her sensual nature and response to him. Earlier she had tried to push him away, now she wanted only to be closer to him, to be one with him. Never had she experienced such pleasure from a man, the slow burn he was creating was every bit as encompassing and compelling as the feral coupling she usually experienced with him. His only goal seemed to be eliciting the maximum response to his attentions. Once again, Flynn could hear and feel her breathing became shallow as electricity flowed through her system. She cried out as her pussy spasmed in need for something much larger and harder than his tongue.

When she'd come back to him, she looked down to see him still cradling her thighs between his arms, his chin resting on her mons as he stared at her intently. A low, grumbling from deep in his throat surrounded her and she heard an answering sound, surprised when she realized the noise was coming from her. Her entire body seem to vibrate with need. He traced slow, deliberate circles around her nipples with his fingertips as he nuzzled her clit. Once again, her body responded to his fondling and teasing. Flynn closed her eyes, reveling in the carnal pleasure he was providing. She refused to think, indulging in the sensations he was causing. She could feel the beginning of another orgasm.

He reversed the direction he had taken earlier and slowly dragged his hard body along her length, nipping, sucking, and kissing his way up. He dragged his hand between her legs which parted easily for him. Alex penetrated her wet heat with first one, and then two fingers. Removing his hand, he rolled on top of her, replacing his digits with his fully engorged cock, sinking to her depths before he groaned in satisfaction. While his hands and mouth had provided her with tremendous pleasure, she ached to feel him fully encased in her sheath before he began stroking her. His tongue and fingers had provided her with great erotic pleasure. His cock took that pleasure and amplified it. He filled her completely as her entire pussy was stroked from its entrance to its end.

Alex was well endowed. The length of his cock was complemented by girth. The entire circumference of her pussy was being stroked in the most exquisite way. Her eyes rolled back in her head and she surged upward to meet him. She almost orgasmed beneath him before he took his first stroke. Grasping her hips, he thrust in and out of her slowly.

As he thrust forward the third time, Flynn came undone beneath him and climaxed, grasping at his back before digging her nails into it. He stilled within her and let her ride the crest of her orgasm without being distracted by anything. When her body stilled, he began his slow stroking again.

"More," she whispered, wrapping her body around his and digging her nails into his back. "Faster. Harder."

Alex moved hard against her. Flynn lost track of time and space; all she could do was feel. He had captured her completely. There was no escape. She could do nothing but respond to him. She knew that he was deliberately taking his time in achieving his own release. His only goal seemed to be how long and hard he could pleasure her before succumbing to his own need to drive deeply and empty himself into her. As he continued to move within her, Flynn's pussy pulsed in the same rhythm as his stroking. She felt another orgasm begin to well up and envelop her as he stroked harder and faster and finally thrust home to empty himself deep within her.

CHAPTER TWELVE

When he rolled off of her, Flynn felt the loss on a myriad of levels. She reflexively reached for him to stay his departure. Leaning down, he kissed her.

"I'm just going to go turn on the shower for you," he said softly.

"Don't," she said, her voice breaking.

"It's okay, Flynn," he said standing and lifting her out of the bed.

Cradling her in his arms, he carried her into their adjoining bathroom and set her on her feet, ensuring that he supported her with one hand as he turned on and adjusted the shower. He stepped into the shower and drew her in with him.

Flynn glanced down and saw nothing that would indicate she'd ever been shot or injured in any way.

"How?" she said running her hand over where the wound should have been.

"I don't suppose you'd buy Bactine and a Band-Aid?"

"Seriously, Alex. I remember a burning sensation and then blood; there was so much blood."

He nodded. "Let's get you washed up. Allie put some shampoo and conditioner in here she thought you might like."

Flynn was confused. Gone was the man/beast whose rough treatment had so inflamed her libido. In his place was the man who was gently bathing her and washing her hair, combing conditioner through it. They enjoyed the hot, pounding water and once clean, got out and dried off.

"Simon wants you to rest up and get back in bed."

"He said he wants me to take it easy. That earlier romp notwithstanding, I want my clothes and I want to go home."

"You are home, Flynn. And you will do as you're told. Now, get back in that bed and stay there."

"I was wondering what happened to the asshole," she quipped.

"Get into bed, Flynn."

She reached for a clean nightgown. "Should I ask who these belong to?"

"Jealous, mate?" he chuckled. "They belong to you. Allie had them sent up once she knew your size. But," he said, seizing it, "you will remain naked in our bed until I am sure you are sufficiently recovered. While I'm gone, if you follow Simon's orders, you can have run of the house, even the village if Yutu or Josh is with you…"

"I am not your mate and you do not get to tell me what I will and won't do," she said, making a grab for the gown.

"You are my mate and there are none here who will dispute it."

"I will dispute it," she snarled.

"You have no say in the matter. I'll go down and get you something to eat. If you are anything other than naked and in our bed when I return, I will punish you for your disobedience."

He turned on his heel and left her standing, naked and alone in the middle of the bedroom.

• • • • • • •

"Did you tell her?" Josh asked as he made his way down

the staircase and into the kitchen.

"We didn't do a lot of talking," said Alex with a self-satisfied smile.

"I'll bet. Which do you think she's going to have the bigger issue with? The fact that you turned her without her consent or that she was unconscious for her own bonding ceremony?"

"Neither is relevant. She is both turned and my mate… her opinion never entered into it."

"I think you will find her opinion matters a great deal. Personally, I think she might give you a pass on the whole being turned thing, but forcing her into a bonding ceremony…"

"But I didn't force her; she didn't object."

"Because she was unconscious! Alex, I understand why you did it, especially turning her…"

"She would have died. As for the bonding, you know as well as I do that Kodiak females often have to be coerced into taking their vows. Now, regardless of what happens to me, she will have the protection of the clan."

"That's not why you did it, and we both know it," accused Josh.

Alex stopped and took a deep breath. "It might not have been the only reason, but it was a determining factor about whether to wait or not. You can assure Allie that one way or another, I would have taken Flynn to mate. And you, little brother, had best figure out how to get through the rut next year, as I plan to make hard and extensive use of my mate."

Shaking his head, Josh sighed. "When do you leave for Seattle?"

"I issued a challenge to Koto immediately upon Yutu's return. I gave the lizard forty-eight hours. I will leave for the Emerald City in the morning. If I do not hear from him by dawn the day after, I will hunt him down and settle things between us. Then, I'll contact Flynn's brother to let him know he can return to his home and invite him to visit us later in the year after I have Flynn more settled."

"How do you plan to deal with Koto—long distance, sniper shot?"

"No, that's too quick and clean. There was a time I might have done that or allowed him to end his own miserable existence. Once he tried to have my mate killed, he ensured that I would give him no easy exit from this life. Anything else? I want to get back up to Flynn."

"Let me know if I can do anything to help."

Alex could feel his brother's eyes on his back as he returned to the bedroom he now shared with Flynn. He transferred the tray loaded with food and drink to one hand and turned the doorknob with the other. It was only opened a fraction when a piece of Inuit pottery crashed against the wall and doorframe. It would seem Flynn's mood had not improved much.

Ducking, he entered their room and placed their food on the dresser just inside the door. She had grabbed one of his red flannel shirts to cover herself with.

"Enough, Flynn," he commanded. "You were told to get back into bed. As you seem well enough to disobey me and destroy a valuable artifact in a fit of temper, shall I assume that you are recovered sufficiently to be punished for doing so?"

"You can't keep me locked in here," she cried.

"So, you tried the windows as well. I suppose that's good as you are now aware that I will do what is necessary to keep you safe. My brother's mate pointed out to me that our bedroom is decidedly masculine, so perhaps you should spend your time while I deal with Koto remaking our nest here in the lodge so that it is more to your liking. Once it is safe, you can do the same to our cabin as well as our den up in the cliff."

"I need to get word to my brother…"

"Your brother is safe. He is in Reykjavík. I just told Josh that I will let him know when he can return to Seattle and that we should invite him later this year."

"You can't just usurp my life."

"I can and have. I plan to head to Seattle in the morning. There are things you need to know before I go. I would have preferred to spend the rest of the time before I leave rutting with you, but I will not have you uninformed."

"What?" she asked suspiciously.

"While you were recovering, I had the bonding ceremony performed…"

"You what? You sonofabitch!"

"Calm yourself, Flynn. It is done. I needed to know that should I not return, your place amongst our clan was secure."

"So you just had me bonded to you? How could you even do that while I was out of it?"

He shrugged his massive shoulders. "I told you, it isn't uncommon for female Kodiaks to be forced to accept being bonded to their mate. Frankly, no one thought much about it. You are my mate, I claimed you and had our bonding sealed."

"Well, unseal it!"

"Only death will dissolve our union. You are my mate, now and forever. Settle yourself with that reality while I am gone. Come have something to eat."

"I'm not hungry."

"I didn't ask if you were. Besides, you must be hungry. Quit being quarrelsome and have some food."

"I don't want it," she said, turning her back on him, going to the large window at the end of the room and crawling up into the window seat.

"You will eat. You need to regain your strength and you can't do that behaving like a petulant child going on a hunger strike because she can't have her way."

"No," she said with a degree of finality.

"You will eat… either now or after I spank you for not doing as you're told. What is it to be, mate?"

She glared at him from across the room before turning her head to look back out the window.

"Flynn, if I have to come get you, I'll put you over my

knee and turn your pretty backside bright red before I ease my resulting lust in your bottom hole."

Flynn blanched, but refused to acknowledge him.

He crossed the room, jerking her off the window seat so that he could sit down on it before pulling her back across his hard thighs. Alex flipped the hem of the shirt up over her back to reveal her very shapely, ivory bottom. While fetching, he meant to ensure it didn't stay that color for long.

Alex raised his hand, bringing it down to connect with her ass in a gratifying manner. He grinned as Flynn yelped and swore. Over and over he spanked her generous globes, watching them become quickly infused with color. Her bottom had a lovely, firm texture that bounced prettily and had just the right amount of give to it. Her skin was cool and smooth to the touch, but as he rained blow after blow in a pattern that covered the entire area, heat radiated off it as he tattooed her behind with the color of his discipline.

"Let me go! You bastard!" she wailed.

"No. I warned you and I don't make idle threats."

Alex continued to land repeated swats to her backside, inflicting a considerable amount of pain. The only sound was that of his hand spanking her ass. His cock stiffened, both from the imposition of his dominance and in anticipation of the good ass-fucking he planned to give her. She may as well learn that not obeying him had consequences she might want to avoid across her backside.

"What did I tell you to do when I went downstairs?" he asked.

Flynn said nothing and so Alex increased the strength and speed of the spanking, giving her little time to recover from one blow before another landed, compounding the effect of each.

"Answer me," he ordered.

"You told me to be naked and in bed."

"Did you do that?"

When only silence answered his question, he ramped up

the severity of her punishment.

"Unless you want me to take a razor strop to your backside and leave you with a set of welts, you'd better answer me. Did you do as you were told?"

"No. Ouch, damn it, Alex, that hurts." He delivered a few more swats before she continued, "I'm sorry."

The sound of submission to his authority was evident in her voice. He ceased spanking her and then patted her now bright red rump with affection and a kind of acceptance of her surrender.

• • • • • • •

Her ass was on fire, but worse was her body's resulting aroused response to his treatment of her. She wondered at the apparent ease he was able to call forth some kind of almost primal need that could only be satisfied by his rough treatment.

He chuckled and she only had a moment to wonder what he found amusing before he penetrated her dripping sheath, plunging his fingers back and forth before withdrawing them. There was no discussion or warning before he plunged them into her bottom hole, finger-fucking her. Flynn wanted to cry out in pain, outrage, or denial but knew that none of them would be entirely true. While his stroking was not gentle, his use of her back passage only stung for a moment before eliciting a delicious, shameful kind of pleasure.

Flynn's body scaled the heights of her wanton desire. Her moans became soft groans as she willingly offered him her ass for his use. She soared to a different plateau and was about to careen over its side when he withdrew his fingers before plunging them into her wet heat and scooping out the natural lubricant he found there.

She wasn't particularly concerned until he stood, dragged her to the end of the four-poster bed and tossed her over the footboard. When he began slathering the viscous honey he'd gathered from her sheath all over his cock, with the majority being used on its head, she became concerned. When she tried to rise, Alex delivered another stinging blow to her rump before pinning her down by the nape of her neck and guiding his cock to the dark rosebud hidden in the cleft of her buttocks. It was only then she realized his intent. She wanted to deny him but was so far gone in her own need that she couldn't form the necessary words.

Glancing over her shoulder she could see both her own lubrication as well as his pre-cum dripping from the end of his cock. A part of her wanted to fight his violation of her in this way, but she knew neither of them saw it that way. For him, it was an exertion of his dominance; and for her, acceptance and capitulation to his authority. Her need to feel him possess her in this last, intimate act of claiming was too great.

"Ask me to take your ass. Admit you know you are mine."

She said nothing but nodded her head. He swatted her again.

"Not good enough, Flynn; say it!" he growled.

"Please?"

She questioned what she was asking for—was it to have him breach her bottom hole, not have to ask him to do it or to stop and let her gather the remnants of her pride before letting her be?

He landed another swat to her tender globes. She tried to evade him, but he held her in place. "Please what, Flynn? You want me to fuck your ass? You want me to stroke your dark channel the way I do your pussy and fill it with my cum? Tell me what you want."

"Yes, damn it!"

"Ask me," he commanded.

"Fuck my ass, Alex, please?" Flynn wailed and then allowed her body to slump in abject surrender.

"Good girl," he crooned.

He leaned over her back as he pressed his cock against the tight ring of muscle that guarded her back passage. He used both of his hands to clutch her hips in a vice-like grip.

"You want your pretty bottom hole fucked?" he asked seductively.

Flynn had lost the ability to speak—her need was too great, her pride and defiance in shambles. All she could do was nod again and pray that it would be enough.

Alex didn't mount her aggressively as he'd done most often. Instead he allowed his cock to enter her slowly but inexorably. He did not seem hurried but continued to push forward inch-by-inch until he had penetrated her fully and the swell of her sore buttocks was hard up against his hips. She felt the stretch from his cock far more in this dark orifice than she had in her pussy. He growled in satisfaction.

Before she could respond, Alex moved inside her. This was not his usual powerful or frenzied stroking, but a more leisurely savoring of her response as her bottom hole learned to accommodate him and accept pleasure from him in this way as well. The slight sting of his having breached her dark passage with his cock for the first time slowly gave way to a new kind of carnality—one she had never known or thought she needed.

Flynn's nipples beaded and ached, and her pussy thrummed in rhythm to his thrusting in her ass. Alex picked up his pace and began driving into her. Her sighs morphed into a kind of deeply felt keening. She grasped the bedcovers and held on for dear life.

"Alex," she cried as every muscle in her body contracted, including those that enveloped his plunging rod.

"Come for me, Flynn. I'm going to fill your bottom hole just like I do your pussy. You need to get used to the idea that I will use whichever of your holes I want for my pleasure."

The pace and rhythm of his fucking increased, exacerbating her response. As she felt him pump his seed into her, she came again, calling his name. Flynn felt his cum as it spurted into her in the same, yet a wickedly, shamefully, different way as when he came in her pussy. When he'd finished, he stayed buried in her ass as she returned to earth from her rapturous flight, or ascended from the depths of her despair, she wasn't sure which.

Alex eased himself from her bottom hole in the same way he'd claimed it—slowly, gently, and in full control. As he left her, she felt his loss and collapsed over the end of the bed. He lifted her and held her as he turned back the covers and deposited her onto the mattress, before returning to the dresser and retrieving the tray.

"Give me the shirt, Flynn," he said, setting the food down on the nightstand.

She said nothing... could not even meet his eyes as he reached over and removed it. How had she let what just happened, happen? Worse, how could she have found pleasure from the act itself or in his treatment of her? She rolled onto her side away from him, curling into a ball. At what point had she begun to crave his touch, whether it was harsh or gentle? Was he right—had some primitive part of her known that she was destined for this creature? In two years, she had been unable to break the bond he had forged that night in the pub. Now she wondered if she even wanted to.

"Sit up, Flynn. You need to eat and there are some things you need to know before I leave in the morning."

"Can't you just leave me alone?" she said softly, feeling broken and betrayed in both body and soul. "I'm tired."

Alex trailed his hand down her spine, caressing her tender backside.

"I probably could," he said, "but there's no reason for me to do so. You need nourishment and we need to talk. You'll have plenty of time to rest once I leave in the morning. You'll have little sleep this night. Hopefully, Koto will not keep me waiting and I can return to you in just a day or two. Once I've eliminated that threat, we'll retreat to our den, up in the cavern, and I'll rut with you for the remainder of the season."

"Is that supposed to be something I look forward to?" Flynn snarked, her normal fire and determination once again asserting themselves.

She moved away from him, snatching the shirt back, rolling up and off the bed into a standing position. The move would have been more impressive had she not winced as her butt slid across the sheets or her knees not threatened to buckle. Flynn pulled the shirt back on and glared at him across the bed.

"Get back in bed. Simon says you are not fully recovered and need to relax," Alex ordered.

"Is that what you call what just happened—relaxing?"

Had she been standing close enough, Flynn would have slapped the smirk right off his face or scratched his eyes out.

"What I call it is disciplining my mate. Unless you'd like another trip over my knee, I suggest you do as you're told."

They stood in what amounted to a Mexican standoff. Flynn briefly wondered why it was referred to that way. Alex said nothing but lifted the cover from several of the dishes on the nightstand. The aroma of the food wafted across the bed, making her stomach grumble. He placed the tray on the bed, gently sliding it across to her. Flynn reached for a chicken leg only to have her hand slapped.

"The shirt, Flynn. I want you naked."

She lifted her in chin in defiance, but before she could make a scathing retort, he continued, "Give me the shirt and eat something. Much as I'd like to do nothing more than rut with you, there are things you need to know."

"You keep saying that. You make whatever it is sound ominous."

"That would depend on how you define ominous. It is serious but shouldn't be frightening."

"I'm not afraid of you," she said.

Alex chuckled. "No, you're afraid of yourself. Eat, Flynn."

"I seem to have lost my appetite."

"I don't much care. You will sit in the middle of our bed naked and eat…"

"Or what?"

"Or I will take a razor strop to your backside and then you'll eat," he snarled.

"I'll eat, but I keep the shirt."

His eyes searched her face and lost some of his angry countenance.

"You, my mate, have tremendous courage. There are few who would openly defy me. Our bloodline will produce Kodiak sons who will be great warriors and our daughters will be coveted as mates within our society."

"Like your brother's?"

"Only if they decide to be turned at some point in the future."

"I don't understand…"

"Josh is Kodiak, but Allie is not. Their children will not have the ability to shift unless they are turned."

"You're taking a rather large leap of faith that we will have kids…"

"As often as you will be bred, offspring are inevitable," he said with a self-satisfied smirk.

Flynn felt her nipples begin to stiffen and her pussy clench in anticipation and arousal. There was something feral and raw about his effect on her.

"But it sounded like you were saying any children we had would be Kodiaks… like you."

"And you," he said quietly.

CHAPTER THIRTEEN

"What do you mean by that?" she asked carefully, crawling up onto the bed and taking a chicken leg, ripping a bit of the meat away from the bone.

"I think you know what I mean," he said levelly.

Flynn set the food back down on the plate. "Why don't you explain it to me?"

"I told you that my mate would be Kodiak and that you were my mate…"

"You mean…"

"Yes, Flynn. You are no longer human. You are Kodiak."

"You bastard! How dare you!"

"I dared because you were dying. Had I not, you would no longer be part of this world."

"Change me back," she seethed.

"That isn't possible, Flynn. I told you that my mate would be Kodiak and that you were my mate. You would have been transitioned in any event. Circumstances meant that it happened sooner rather than later."

"And without my agreeing to it."

He snorted. "Your agreement wasn't necessary."

"It was for me," she said, heaving the entire tray of food

at him.

Alex stepped back and swatted the flying objects away from his face. Flynn leaped over the end of the bed, flinging the bedroom door open and charging down the hall and then the stairs. She bowled Josh over as he tried to block her escape. Alex's brother grabbed her arm, trying to use her inertia to spin her back toward the interior of the house.

Rage fueled by fear and adrenaline flooded her system; she roared at him, making a bid for freedom through the front door. She stumbled as Josh managed to divert her away from her goal. Flynn felt something shudder and shift within her—great strength surged forward. She barely registered the sound of cloth being rendered. She brought her hand up to break his hold. When she lifted her hand to bat his hand away, she couldn't believe her eyes. There, before her eyes, was the massive paw of a Kodiak bear... complete with razor-sharp claws. She watched with a kind of detached fascination as his flesh was torn apart as easily as the sleeve of the shirt.

Her steps only faltered for a moment as she growled at him.

"Flynn," Alex said charging down the steps. "Stop it."

She galloped out of the main living area towards what appeared to be the kitchen. She barreled through the closed, exterior door, not bothering to stop to try to open it. Flynn crashed through the strong, wooden barrier as if it were no more than spiderwebs. She raced outside, turning away from the sea water, lapping gently against the pebbled shore. She galloped into the main square of the village. She could hear Alex's angry bellow as she stampeded past surprised onlookers, sprinting towards the woods that appeared to surround the compound.

Flynn was accelerating and thought she might be able to get away. Her hope and half-formed plan were shattered as a larger, more powerful paw swiped her hip, knocking her off of her feet. She tumbled along the ground but regained her feet, turning to snarl at Alex. She knew it was Alex.

Something fundamental in her being would have recognized him regardless of the shape he was in. She saw a barely discernible shimmer as his naked human form shifted back into being.

"Call your humanity forward and do it now," he ordered.

Her response was to roar at him, taking a swipe at his broad, brawny chest.

Alex jumped back, just out of reach, "Knock it off, Flynn. Shift back or I will shift again and show you what it is to be mate to an enraged alpha male. You will not find pleasure in that. Now, Flynn," he bellowed.

Recognition that she did not know how she shifted and therefore did not know how to shift back spread across his features. Fear of what might happen if she shifted back flooded her being—fear combined with desire.

"Calm your mind and call your human self forward. The bear will recede and relinquish her hold on you. I promise you will not like it if I have to force the shift back."

She wondered if he recognized the difficulty involved in doing as he said. Closing her eyes, she tried to slow her racing thoughts. She felt her bear begin to leave her conscious mind, but was reassured when she could still feel her. Glancing down, she watched as her paw became a human hand again.

Flynn was quite certain she had never seen anything as arousing as Alex standing naked in the sunlight—legs spread, arms crossed over his chest and his cock rising to a state of readiness. It was as if she was mesmerized by the sight of him. She couldn't look away. He was so enticing, so compelling.

Remaining on all fours, Flynn crawled to him, nuzzling his groin as her small, pink tongue darted out to lick the underside of his cock. She wasn't expecting him to fist her hair and drive his rigid shaft past her lips, driving to the back of her throat. She suppressed her gag reflex, relaxed her jaw and accepted his staff as he groaned heavily.

Flynn began using all of her skill to please him as she

licked and sucked his entire length. She took a kind of pride when he relaxed the hold he had of her hair and stroked it instead. Alex rocked his hips back and forth. He groaned and Flynn felt her own need begin to assert itself. She could feel his anger, rolling off of him in waves; her pussy quivered in response. She had no doubt about how this would end… precisely the way she wanted it to.

"That feels good, Flynn. More than that, I can smell your arousal. That's good because I have no intention of sending my load into your belly."

Alex closed his eyes and lifted his face to the sun as he grasped both sides of her head to still her movement as he slowly fucked her mouth. The surging ebb and flow of his cock and the appreciative sounds of male pleasure kept Flynn focused on the job at hand. Normally when she was blowing a man, she felt in control, but she was acutely aware that Alex was in complete and utter control of the situation. Alex's controlled movements left no doubt as to who was servicing whom. His pleasure advanced her state of arousal—her nipples were becoming painfully hard and wet desire pooled in her core, awaiting his use.

He arched his back, fucking her face harder and making her gag. He ignored it and plunged deeper into her mouth. It was as if he was trying to shove his cock all the way down her throat. His fingers tightened in her hair and he bucked his hips harder. His staff twitched and swelled as his release became imminent. With no warning, he pulled out of her mouth, but held her in place on her knees, stepping behind her. He forced her torso down, spreading her legs as he knelt behind her—his cock nudging her labia as it sought the entrance to her core. Alex surged forward and Flynn moaned in response, teetering on the edge of orgasm.

Of the men she had fucked before Alex, none had been so willing to ignore every social norm and barrier. It occurred to her to glance around, as they were out in the open and might not be alone. His hard thrusting refocused her on him and his dominant coupling with her. Nothing beyond pure animal lust drove them both into a frenzy of fucking as she arched her back, spreading her legs wider and offering him easier access to her cunt. His enormous cock impaled her as he thrust, stretching her repeatedly.

She panted at the same speed and rhythm that he hammered her pussy. Flynn felt every ridge and vein of his staff as it ravaged her inner walls. She moaned as he took her, feeling her own orgasm rapidly approaching. Alex released her hair as he grasped both of her hips and drove into her with increased speed and power, grunting with every stroke.

Her muscles seized as she tumbled into the void where no questions remained; just the certain knowledge that this man completed her, that she had been created for him alone and that regardless of what happened in the future, her destiny was intertwined with his. From the distance of the abyss of ecstasy she heard a scream of erotic pleasure and only barely recognized the voice as hers.

Her pussy clamped down hard, trying to trap his cock as it pounded inside her. Flynn keened her need and satisfaction as her sheath shuddered all along his length. Alex gave a last, brutal thrust as he drove home, flooding her pussy with his hot seed. She felt it bathing her inner walls, coating it with its sticky substance as he spurted the last of it close to her cervix. Flynn collapsed, uncoupling herself from him. She was exhausted past the point of all reason. He fisted her hair as he stood, drawing her up beside him. She felt his semi-erect cock still wet from their mating at the apex of her thighs. He leaned down, tossing her over the apex of his torso, before standing up and striding back to their lodge.

Flynn was only vaguely aware that she was naked, slung over her mate's broad shoulder being paraded back through the village before the eyes of their clan. Mate? Their clan? When had she begun to think that way, she asked herself. The answer came swiftly—right about the time she went down on him and then allowed him to mount and fuck her on her knees in the dirt where anyone could have seen them.

He entered the house and instead of going up the stairs to their bedroom, he strode into the kitchen, lugging her along as though she were a sack of grain. Alex landed a hard strike on her exposed backside.

"Apologize to Josh; you clawed him pretty good."

"Oh, God, Josh! Are you all right? Did I hurt you too badly?" she cried, rising up from the position in which Alex had her, truly mortified at the damage she must have inflicted.

"I'm fine," said Josh in an amiable tone. "Kodiak physiology means we heal rapidly. All I had to do was clean it up a bit and it was well on the way to being healed. By tonight, you'll never be able to see I was injured at all. Are you all right?"

Her answer was cut off when Alex's hand struck her again. "My mate is fine. She's been well fucked and her cunt is full of my seed. I plan to spend the rest of what time is left before I have to leave doing more of the same."

Alex left Josh standing in the kitchen. Flynn wished she hadn't looked up to see his face. She expected him to look shocked, disgusted, embarrassed, maybe even insulted, but no; the look on his face was one of all-encompassing amusement.

"Help me!" she cried.

"Sure, a friendly piece of advice. Don't piss him off. He's a nasty bastard when he's pissed. I suspect fucking him long, hard, and repeatedly will do a lot to keep him in good mood for which all of us will be grateful," Josh offered, trying hard not to laugh, but failing.

Alex swatted her again. "I'd listen to him if I were you."

She was jostled around, slumped over his shoulder as he trotted up the stairs and walked down to their room, opening the door and dumping her unceremoniously on the bed.

"Now that your tantrum is over…'

"Tantrum? You come barging into my life…"

"If I hadn't, you'd be dead, at least three times so far…"

"That is not pertinent to this discussion."

His laugh caught her off guard as he pulled on a pair of jeans. He indicated a new tray of food. "Eat. Shifting takes its toll on your body. You need to replenish your strength especially since you are so recently recovered from a nearly fatal wound and going through the transition."

"What fatal wound?" she asked tentatively, as her mind worked to recall something at the outermost limits of her memory.

"Try and calm your breathing, Flynn. Becoming agitated will not serve you well. As you recently discovered, if your bear feels you are in danger, whether or not your assessment of the situation is correct, and you let slip your control, she will come forward to protect you."

Fascinated, she asked, "Do I have to be upset in order to shift?"

"No. You can learn to call her forward anytime you choose. For example, if you need to get from point A to point B over rough terrain, it is often easier to do so as a bear. Normally, you plan for it and remove your clothing, placing them into a bundle and taking them with you."

Her anger over his treatment of her reared its ugly head. "None of which negates that you imposed this weird kind of double existence on me. You gave me no choice."

"You're right, I didn't. But I had no choice either—you were bleeding out. The only way I could keep you from dying was to initiate the change and pray that it would save you, which it did."

"I… I was dying?"

He nodded. "In the warehouse, Koto's assassins shot you, which I might point out they would have been unable to do had you stayed up in our den."

"But you planned to do it before I was shot…"

"Yes, to make you one with me. You are now Kodiak—stronger, more resilient, faster, more able to adapt to harsh environments, harder to kill."

"And now bonded to you as your mate…"

He laughed again. "I think that bothers you a whole lot less than being Kodiak."

He stopped speaking and leaned back against the dresser thoughtfully, resting his butt on the piece of furniture and bracing against it with only his heels on the floor.

Slowly, he began speaking again, as if measuring his words. "I don't want you to think for even a minute that I wouldn't have turned you without your consent, but I would have tried to persuade you and would have prepared you. But I didn't have a choice. Simon said you would have died and that was unacceptable. As it was, we almost lost you. It was only the combination of Simon's skill and the infusion of Kodiak blood that saved you."

"But why me?" she asked, dropping the hostility.

He shrugged. "Because you are my mate. I knew it before I ever touched you in Seattle." He snorted a derisive laugh. "I can assure you I don't normally sidle up to a woman and finger fuck her in a crowded bar and then take her into the back to mate with her for the first time."

"But the second or third time would be okay?" she quipped, the first hint of humor and acceptance in her voice. "I guess there's some comfort in that. What about my brother?"

"What about him? Tell your brother whatever you wish to. I only spoke briefly with Ben, but I know he would never do anything to harm you, so I believe our secret would be safe. I don't want you to feel like you have to keep any secrets."

He rocked back up onto his feet and came towards her. "You, my beautiful mate, call to me in a way no other ever has. In the past, the rut has always been, for me, an undeniable physical need once a year to spend a week or two fucking a wet cunt—any wet cunt. With you, my need goes far beyond that. There is so much more to experience as a shifter, and I want to share all of that with you… and only you."

She could see in his eyes and his body language that the admission had cost him. Part of her said she ought to leave him out on that fragile limb to twist slowly in the wind, but the better part of her knew he was her mate and she couldn't do that to him.

Rocking up onto her knees, she crawled towards the edge of the bed, reaching out to wrap her arms around his neck and draw him forward.

"You might have led with that… mate," she whispered, before allowing her body to meld with his and kiss him with the quiet intensity of a distant storm.

Alex groaned as he returned the embrace, pulling her close and seizing control of the kiss. The kiss was different from the few he had inflicted before. While still passionate and dominant, it was more of an exploration of her response. Instead of demanding, it was coaxing… and all the more compelling because of it. They stood for several minutes doing nothing more—or less—than kissing before he broke it off.

"You are far too enticing," he said quietly.

"Is that such a bad thing for one's mate to be?" she asked seductively.

"It is when you really do need to eat. I think it would be better if you got dressed and we joined the rest of the family for a meal. I fear if I stay up here with you naked and willing, you will prove too tempting."

"Family? Oh shit, Alex, your nieces could have seen us."

"No, I knew the girls were out with their mother and that the only one home was Josh."

"Hmm, yes, Josh. You won't be angry if I hit him over the head with something for not helping me."

He chuckled. "While I applaud the thought and can see your point of view, I would point out that you did open up his arm when you clawed him. I think you should call it a draw and be thankful I don't punish you for such behavior."

"I would think you'd be far more interested in fucking me than spanking me."

"First, the two aren't mutually exclusive. I assure you there will be many times you get fucked with a red, swollen, painful bottom. Second there are a variety of ways other than spanking that I can punish you."

She searched his face. "Damn, you're serious."

"Very. If you behave downstairs, I will consider that matter closed as well as all of your previous misbehavior. We can start with a clean slate. Agreed?"

She got off the bed and walked to the chest to rummage through them, pulling on a pair of leggings and one of Alex's sweaters.

"No shoes or socks?" he asked.

"No, I've always preferred going barefoot, which I suppose is a far more appropriate and applicable term than it was two weeks ago. And Ben is safe?"

"He is. You can call him if you like."

She nodded, throwing back over her shoulder as she opened the door and went out in the hall. "I'd like to do that before we return to Seattle."

"*We* won't be returning to Seattle… at least not for some time. *I* will leave in the morning to deal with Koto…"

"I'm the one he tried to kill," she said as they made their way down the stairs.

"And almost succeeded in doing so," he said, leaving no doubt in her mind that he considered the matter closed. "You will remain here where our clan can keep you safe."

They entered the dining room just as food was being laid out.

"He hired people before, what makes you think he'll face you alone?" she asked.

"He has no choice," he answered. "The Komodo Tribunal, their governing body, has decreed this to be personal between Koto and me. The Komodos want no part of a war with Kodiaks. They indicated they would advise his clutch not to back anything he might want them to do. I agreed if the tribunal and the clutch stayed out of it, I would confide my justice to Koto himself."

"And if he wants peace… you know, let bygones be bygones?"

Alex shook his head as he held out a chair, indicating she should sit between him and his eldest niece.

"Too much has been done. Henry almost killed Josh; Kevin and David tried to kill you. The Kotos don't get to do that and live."

"What about just regular justice—like with cops and lawyers."

"Koto has too much money; he'll just buy himself an acquittal." He leaned down to give her a chaste kiss and whispered, "No, Koto will die."

Dinner was a lively affair. Flynn could easily imagine Ben sitting among them at the holidays. She knew Alex would demand that she rearrange her life to suit him, and oddly, that didn't bother her nearly as much as it should have.

After dinner, they remained downstairs and Flynn took the time to get to know her two new nieces and their mother.

When Josh and Alex took the girls out for a kayak ride, Allie and Flynn both begged off.

"Can you tell them apart yet?" asked Allie. "It took me a while, but then I didn't get to see them together a lot at first. Alex used to scare the hell out of me."

"He can be a scary sonofabitch when he wants to be, but yes, Alex is a couple of inches taller, carries more muscle, and his features are more angular."

"Josh is quicker to laugh. He and I both hope that will change now that he's brought you home. Talk about a bad mood… every time he came back from Seattle after that first time you met. Did you know he was looking for you?"

Flynn nodded. "I did. Somehow, I figured if he came back looking for me, it would be at the same time of the year. However, I never connected it to Kodiak mating season."

"And you're all right with all of this?" Allie asked her.

"Surprisingly, yes," Flynn laughed and knew it to be true.

"Maybe it's the Kodiak DNA, but what a couple of days ago would have been weird… like Twilight Zone weird… now seems normal and in a funny way as if it was always supposed to be this way."

Allie smiled. "Josh is worried about him…"

"He thinks I'll break his brother's heart?"

"No. I think there was a part of Josh that worried about that until earlier this afternoon. He said that between you becoming Kodiak and just the way Alex carried you in… he figured you two were going to be okay. He's worried about this confrontation with Koto."

"Look, Allie, we haven't known each other for very long, but I'm not big on mincing words. Alex isn't going to have a confrontation with Koto. He means to kill him. I saw him deal with the other two brothers and know what he did with the assassins Koto sent to kill us. David Koto doesn't stand a chance."

"I don't doubt that. Alex is a formidable opponent when he doesn't give a damn, but to protect his family? His mate? There's no way he doesn't come out on top. Josh just worries about the cost to his soul. Alex was a sniper during the war; it changed him. In some ways it made him a better clan leader, but I'm not sure he'll be the easiest guy to live with."

Flynn laughed. "That might be the understatement of the year. He tends to be a bit over-the-top in the dominant, alpha-male category and I worry that he wants someone who wants to just fall in line and that's not me."

"Make no mistake. Alex wants you. There are plenty of females—Kodiak and human alike who would willing flop on their backs and spread their legs…"

"Not a visual I needed."

"Come on, even I can feel the guy's sexual magnetism, but my point was he didn't want any of them. He wanted you. I don't know that he's even looked at another woman since that incident at the pub. He may have taken the edge off at some of the clubs over on the mainland during mating season, but I think that may have only been after he returned when he thought he could get you out of his system."

Flynn blushed. "You know about the pub?"

"Only enough to know it affected him deeply. And what I will tell you is that male Kodiaks pretty much have a gut instinct about who their mate is and are willing to go all out to get her on board with the idea."

"But?" asked Flynn.

"I don't know. I guess I just wanted you to know if you need my help, I'm here. He didn't ask for your consent about turning you and he had you bonded to him when you were unconscious."

"I understand my choice about becoming Kodiak was for him to turn me or I died. Considering how good I feel, Kodiak seems better than dead. As for the bonding thing… I agree with you, but when I really think about it, it's more that he did it that way than I don't want to be with him."

Allie nodded. "Good, but to your earlier point? I don't think he wanted a submissive mate."

"My butt would tell you otherwise."

"Perhaps, but I think he likes that you're strong, tough, and can and will stand up to him."

"He says I'll give him strong sons and daughters that will be sought after," laughed Flynn.

Allie joined her. "That too. He does worry about their bloodline. Our girls aren't Kodiak and won't be unless they choose to be."

"Would you be opposed to that?"

"Not if it's what they want."

"And you never wanted it?"

"I could never make up my mind and I figured unless I was very sure then it was better not to do it. Josh has always been okay with it even though I know Alex feels differently. I hope now that he has you, he'll cut Josh some slack."

Flynn laid her hand on Allie's arm. "I'll see if I can't help with that. As for needing your help, I may take you up on that. I don't want Alex going to Seattle alone and I know he's tasked Josh with staying here and ensuring the rest of the clan is safe."

"I would point out you are a part of the clan and your safety is paramount to him."

Flynn looked her square in the face. "As his is to me."

Allie grinned. "It would seem the Unangan Clan has another female warrior as Lady of the Clan. Yutu's mate, Lena, knows how to fly a seaplane. We can get you out."

"You know, Allie, I think you and I are going to be the best of friends."

CHAPTER FOURTEEN

When Alex returned to the lodge, Allie told him Flynn had gone up to their room. Taking the steps two at a time, he opened the door, stopped short and then entered slowly, closing and locking the door behind him. Flynn was propped up on her back—naked, beaded nipples, legs spread and the entrance to her core wet and inviting. His cock became engorged and throbbed in anticipation. He meant to fuck her all night. She'd get a taste of what it was to be rutted. Come tomorrow, she'd be sore and more likely not to give Josh and Yutu a hard time while he was gone.

Without uttering a single word, Alex stripped out of clothes before joining her at the side of the bed. He palmed her breasts before climbing onto the mattress, lowering himself between her thighs and mounting her with one, hard plunge to her depths. Flynn reached up and clutched at him as she came hard from nothing more than him ramming his cock home. Her legs wrapped around his and he settled into a strong rhythm of thrusting, groaning as he did.

He stroked her, feeling her pussy quiver and tried to remember if there had ever been a time he'd enjoyed fucking a woman even half this much. He reached under her and took hold of her ass to hold her steady so he could extract the maximum amount of pleasure she could give him.

Flynn's breathing sped up and lost its rhythm. She panted shallowly in unison with his grunting as he plowed her. Alex focused on the way she was responding in order to keep himself from spilling himself too soon. He felt her body begin to stiffen in anticipation of her impending climax. She threw her head back and keened in both need and fulfillment. He thrust ferociously into her hot, wet heat, reveling in the way she writhed beneath him. Alex roared his own satisfaction as she clung to him, whimpering as her pussy spasmed and trembled all along his cock as he pumped his seed deep inside her. His orgasm took an eternity to end and Flynn clutched him as her cunt rolled through a series of mini-climaxes, encouraging him to deposit every last drop of his cum and stay coupled with her.

When he'd finished, he rolled off of her and nudged her onto her side, wrapping one massive arm around her, pulling her body into his. Alex reached up to idly to play with both of her nipples and trailed down the midline of her body to stroke her clit. She moaned and snuggled back into his body, offering him no resistance. He had ensured Flynn would be sore tomorrow. She needed to become accustomed to his tremendous need for her, especially during the mating season. Given the level of her response, he no longer worried that she would not welcome the rut as much as he. Settling himself against her, he stopped caressing her but left his hand in place to cup her entire mons. She belonged to him and nothing would ever threaten her again.

• • • • • • •

Flynn's eyes fluttered open. She felt the loss of his presence in the bed. She rolled to her back and stretched languorously.

"I'd watch putting yourself in that position during the rut," he said smiling as he walked out of the bathroom, crossed over to her, and leaned down to kiss her as he tickled her clit. He ended the kiss by nuzzling her neck. "Behave yourself while I'm gone."

"Do you have to leave? Maybe if we just stay up here, he'll leave us alone."

"And are you suggesting that your brother stay in Reykjavík?"

He kissed her, silencing her before she could protest.

"Dealing with Koto will not keep me long from between your thighs," he said caressing them.

He moved away from her and dressed quickly, pulling a wide, well-worn belt through the loops of his jeans.

"I know Seattle better than you. I could help," she argued softly.

"If you leave the village, for any reason, I'll take this belt to your backside and welt your ass until rutting with me will be a combination of pain and pleasure."

"You're an overbearing sonofabitch, you know that?"

He leaned back and kissed her again. "So I've been told. But I am your mate and your clan leader, and you will remain here and stay safe. Try not to be too much of a pain in the ass while I'm gone."

"Love you too," she quipped.

That stopped him short at the door. Turning back, he said, "Do you?"

She smiled. "Yes, I do. And I'll wanted it recorded in the history of our clan that I said it first."

He grinned at her. "Duly noted."

He left their room; Flynn heard him trot down the stairs, whistling a happy tune. She only hoped that he wouldn't be furious with her the next time they shared a bed. Rising up out of the bed, she pulled on the shirt he had discarded the night before and walked out onto their balcony, waving as the plane he was in taxied away from the dock and took to the skies.

"Come in," she called when she heard a knock on her door.

"Do you kayak?" asked Allie.

Flynn turned to her, "I do. Why?"

"Lena has a seaplane waiting around the point. Fastest way there is kayak. Yutu has the girls and I'm going to keep Josh busy so you can make your escape."

"How much trouble am I getting the two of you into?"

"Not enough that we don't have your back. You know Seattle far better than he does. I think he needs you in his corner. He needs to know he can't exclude you. And I doubt anyone could stop you."

Flynn flashed her a grin. "Your grasp of the situation is excellent. I'll be ready to go in a few minutes. I take it my escape kayak is the red one down there?"

"That would be the one. Good luck, Flynn."

"I don't need luck, Allie. I have Alex."

She dressed quickly and waited for the house to grow quiet again. Slipping out, she jogged down to the dock, untied the kayak and paddled out into the bay before turning to the left and making her way around the point. The seaplane and Lena were waiting. She grounded the kayak and boarded.

• • • • • • •

Alex was a bit surprised when there was a man holding a sign with his name on it waiting outside the TSA checkpoint.

"I'm Alex Kingston."

"Thank you, sir. I have a call for you," he said, handing him a cell phone.

"Ranger Kingston?" said the female voice he thought he recognized as that of Koto's executive assistant.

"Yes?"

"A message from my employer. Space Needle

Observation Deck tonight at 2 AM. The security code for the elevator is 3-4-5-3. Do I need to repeat that?"

"No, 3-4-5-3."

"Very good. Mr. Koto hopes you can conclude your business this evening without further hostilities."

"Doubtful, but thank you for the information."

Alex wouldn't need the code. He planned to be there long before the Needle closed and lie in wait for his adversary. He wanted this over and done with. His cock was uncomfortable, and he wanted to be back with Flynn as soon as possible.

• • • • • • •

Normally, Flynn was asleep on an airplane before it ever reached cruising altitude, but she was agitated and couldn't get comfortable. She told herself it was because Alex had left her deliberately sore, but she knew that wasn't it. She was worried for Alex. It had taken her entire life to find him and she had no intention of losing him to some reptilian thug and his minions.

Her plane had been delayed and she failed to reach her houseboat until after dark. Making sure she was secure, she called Koto's office, talking her way through a series of underlings until she was able to speak with his executive assistant.

"Ms. Montgomery, I'm surprised to hear from you."

"I'll bet you are. I need to know where your boss is meeting Alex Kingston."

"I'm afraid I can't supply you with that information," the assistant said in a cool, detached manner.

"Let me explain something to you, blondie. The tribunal and his clutch have turned their backs on him. If I can head Alex off, maybe, just maybe, your boss gets to live. If not, Alex will kill him, skin him, and make a pair of boots out of him."

There was a long pause.

"I know Mr. Koto is expecting him at 2 AM at the Space Needle. That's all I can tell you."

Flynn hung up and dialed her brother.

"Flynn, is that you?" he asked.

"Yes. Are you all right?"

"I am. I spoke with Alex Kingston. He says the two of you are together and that David Koto may be gunning for both of us."

"We are and he is. Don't you have a buddy who works security for the Space Needle?"

"Yeah… but this is a lot more complicated and dangerous than you might understand."

She grinned. She didn't know how, but she suspected that somehow her brother knew—either about the Komodos, the Kodiaks, or both.

"Then you know a fight between a Komodo and my mate will result in one of them dying. Alex is noble and courageous, and Koto will use that against him."

"You know?" Ben asked.

"I do. A more interesting question for later is, how do you? Why don't you see about getting to Kodiak and I can introduce you to the rest of the clan."

"Damn," Ben swore softly. "But you're okay?"

"The sooner I get Alex back up to the village and into our bed, the better. I need the security code to get into the Needle's complex."

"I don't know, Flynn…"

"Ben, I don't have the time to climb the damn Needle. Get me that code and call me back."

Within the hour, she had changed to all black clothing and footwear that would be useful in achieving her goal. As she looked in the mirror she started to laugh. Most likely she would need to discard her clothing and shift to be able to help Alex.

∙∙∙∙∙∙∙

Alex watched from his secure location as the two men working for Koto secreted themselves on the observation deck. The Needle closed for the evening and Alex waited. Shortly before 2 AM, Koto appeared and spoke briefly with those in his employ. Alex moved silently along the deck's outer rim and locked off the elevator system. The only way off the top of the Space Needle was down the long staircase that was part of the interior structure.

At 2 AM sharp, Alex stepped out into the dim light to confront Koto.

• • • • • • •

As Flynn feared, both elevators appeared to be non-operational. She quickly used the key code given to her by her brother to access the stairwell inside the Needle. She removed her clothing using the backpack she had brought with her, ensuring the gun was still on top. She stilled her mind and called forth her bear that flowed smoothly from deep within her to transfigure her physical being. Flynn picked up her bundle and began galloping up the stairs. Climbing over five hundred feet would have been incredibly taxing on her human body, but her bear seemed to enjoy the exercise. She reached the top of the staircase and left her clothing on the landing outside the door to the observation deck. Quietly, she opened the door.

Koto and Alex appeared to be in mortal combat. Koto shifted to his reptilian form and sank his teeth into Alex's forearm. Alex roared as his bear sprang forth and he tossed the lizard away from him,

Koto shifted back as he hit the ground, screaming, "Help me, you bastards! Get him!"

Alex, too, reverted to human as the other two men attacked. Flynn flinched as she heard bones breaking and joints cracking. Koto's goons appeared to be getting the best of Alex, and Koto, himself, now seemed to be closing in for the kill. Alex was trapped against the banister of the observation deck close to one of the few openings.

The air around Koto shimmered and the man became Komodo, his assassins following suit. Their tails wagged slowly back and forth as their jaws snapped together with a sound that seemed to split the night sky. Koto reared up on his hind legs, slashing at Alex with his gigantic claws. Realizing that Koto meant to force Alex over the edge, Flynn charged the distance between them, hitting Koto broadside and knocking him close to the safety railing. Alex quickly grabbed the enormous lizard's back legs and boosted him over the side. They both watched in fascinated horror as Komodo became man once more before he hit the ground.

Alex turned on the two remaining Komodos who shifted back.

"Please, wait. Koto was the leader of a large clutch. The decision was made not to abandon him in his quest for revenge, even though the tribunal urged us to do so. We were told if he lost the fight, to beg you for mercy and peace with what is left of those here in Seattle."

"Why should I let you go?" asked Alex evenly. "Your tribunal gave me carte blanche to deal with the lot of you with no repercussions for my clan."

"But we are no longer a threat to you," said the second assailant. "And you did not come alone as you agreed."

Alex barked a laugh. "Neither did your boss. My mate has joined me against my express orders, something she will answer for later this morning. What is your excuse? Money? Just following orders?"

"No, we are brothers from the Island of Flores. The Koto brothers purchased our sister as their mate. We agreed to help Koto if he would release our sister. No one else would help him and it was the only way we could free her."

"Flynn, go get dressed. Did you bring your clothes up to the top of the stairs?"

She nodded.

"Then do as you're told." He turned to face the

remaining Komodos. "How do I know you can be trusted to honor your word?"

"There are people who will clean up this mess and make it appear that Koto, in his grief over the deaths of his brothers, threw himself from the Space Needle. The plan is already in place. We only need to activate it."

Flynn left the door from the stairwell propped open so she could hear them talking while she dressed. Once she was human and clothed, she rejoined Alex who greeted her with a hard kiss and an even harder swat to her backside.

"My mate and I will leave first. On our way down I will call my brother. If they don't hear from us by 9 AM or we don't see the story of Koto's suicide plastered all over the internet and airwaves, it will be considered an act of war and Clan Unangan will hunt all of you down until there is nothing left of either clutch. Agreed?"

Both men bowed their heads. Flynn thought how puny and pathetic they looked standing naked and shrunken before Alex's robust masculinity. She had to suppress a grin... even now she could feel her nipples getting stiff underneath her bra as desire swirled in her belly.

"It is agreed, and we thank you for your benevolence," said the smaller of the two men.

"See that I don't regret it," Alex said, taking Flynn firmly by the arm and cautiously retreating off of the observation deck and down the staircase.

He phoned Josh, putting him on the speakerphone, to let him know that the feud between the Komodos and the Kodiak appeared to be over, but related the contingency plan to him.

"And Flynn? Jesus, Alex... Allie and Lena conspired with her, and I'm pretty damn sure she's headed for you."

"My mate is here at my side. I never should have tasked you with keeping her under house arrest. If there is a next time, I will take her up to my den, chain her to the bedpost, and leave guards to keep her safe."

"I'm sorry. I never thought... well, it doesn't matter

what I thought. I will tell you that yours won't be the only one nursing a bruised backside in the morning."

Alex laughed. "Good for you and see that both of them get strapped at least three times for me."

"Already done, big brother. Both ladies are feeling quite contrite about having helped the lady of our clan defy our leader."

Flynn said, "Josh, I hope you and Yutu weren't too harsh with them. They only did it to help me. Also, you should know that my brother is en route to Kodiak Island, someone could go pick him up at the airport. And I think he knows about our kind."

Alex nodded. "I wondered if he didn't. Josh, get Ben picked up and we will join you tomorrow."

Alex disconnected before his brother could respond. They made their way out of the stairwell right before a woman's scream split the night. They looked across to where David Koto's remains lay splattered on the hard ground outside the Space Needle.

Alex escorted her to the car and Flynn drove them to the airport. They caught the first flight out and were back on Shuyak within twenty-four hours of leaving the Aleutian Islands.

The Komodos held up their end of the bargain. By the time they were wheels down on Kodiak, David Koto's tragic suicide was all over the news. Alex called Josh and told him he wanted a few days alone with Flynn to rut, but they would then join the rest of the family, now including Ben, at the village. Alex was relatively quiet and solicitous as they journeyed back to their den. As soon as he rolled the door back into place he rounded on her, fisting her hair and propelling her to their bed where he sat down, stripped her of her clothing and draped her over his hard, muscular thigh—his cock pressing against his jeans, trying to get out.

"Alex, please?"

"No, Flynn, I warned you."

"I saved your life…"

"While risking your own and disobeying me. As being spanked by hand has not curbed your rebelliousness, I plan to take my belt to your backside and see if several welts cannot put you in the proper, obedient frame of mind."

Flynn yowled. She had thought her chances of getting spanked were roughly fifty/fifty. She now feared that this preliminary spanking would not be the worst of it.

"You welt me, you sonofabitch, and I'll…"

"You'll what, continue to misbehave so that I give you additional welts? And when I'm through welting your pretty backside, I'm fairly sure you will be wetter than you normally are. Something I plan to take full advantage of."

Flynn couldn't help wailing as he continued to spank her buttocks in earnest—ensuring that every inch was covered. The worst part wasn't the spanking itself but the knowledge that he was most likely right. Her body responded in the same primal way it always did. He landed blow after blow without respite or even letting her catch her breath. Finally, he stopped and she thought he was about to ease the ache in her nether regions.

Instead, she felt him shift her body so that he could unbuckle his belt. Flynn realized this was not the first step in his fucking her and tried to wriggle away from him. He had a firm grasp of her, holding her in place as he freed his belt, whipping it away from his body with a flourish and catching the other end to form a doubled-up loop.

"And now, my mate, you will feel the full force of my displeasure."

He brought the belt down across her reddened backside, leaving a trail of fire in its wake. Flynn screamed at the agony it left behind. Four more times Alex laid a welt across her upturned buttocks, leaving angry, red weals.

When he was done, he helped her up off his knee, not bothering to dry her tears.

"Get into position, Flynn. Present your pussy to me to be rutted."

Flynn crawled onto the bed and stretched herself down

with her legs spread and her pussy exposed not only for his view, but for his use. Alex mounted her in one swift, sure, and powerful move. She felt his pelvis slam into her punished and welted backside as he surged forward, leaning down to grasp the nape of her neck in his teeth. Her response was as primitive as it was compelling; she cried out his name as she orgasmed.

Alex pistoned his hips so that his cock hammered her pussy. As rough as he had been in the past, he was rougher, and she surprised herself by welcoming it. She yowled as he pumped his hips, which seemed only to inflame his lust. If the man behind her was part beast, then she was too, as she only wished to fuck. His hold on her neck tightened as he thrust more deeply within her. He fucked her through two more climaxes as his cock ravaged her interior walls.

"You—will—do—as—you're—told!" he said, punctuating each word with a slap of his hips against her welted backside.

The feelings of passion and being possessed were intense and she gave up the need to do anything other than respond. Over and over he stroked her slit with a fierce and overwhelming need to not only rut with her but to claim her completely. He gave a final ferocious thrust and took hold of her hips to hold her in place as he pumped his seed deep into her cunt.

He remained tight against her ass with her neck in his mouth until he had rendered his last drop and then simply remained inside her. Finally, he withdrew and rubbed the opening to her gaping pussy.

Flynn spent the next few days in bed with Alex reveling in the throes of the rut. Alex rarely left her side and then only to fetch them food. He fucked her with a relentlessness she gloried in and she found her pussy ached for his use when it wasn't wrapped around his cock.

She awakened to find him gone and the door to their den open. Flynn got out of bed gingerly, finding one of his shirts to put on and to pad out to the opening in the cliffside. Hearing her, he turned and smiled.

"Trouble?" she asked scanning the one-hundred-and-eighty-degree perimeter.

He laughed, but shook his head, hugging her to his side to comfort and reassure her.

"Do you know that's what those bartenders called you the night we met?" he asked. "How could I have known how right they were."

THE END

STORMY NIGHT PUBLICATIONS WOULD LIKE TO THANK YOU FOR YOUR INTEREST IN OUR BOOKS.

If you liked this book (or even if you didn't), we would really appreciate you leaving a review on the site where you purchased it. Reviews provide useful feedback for us and for our authors, and this feedback (both positive comments and constructive criticism) allows us to work even harder to make sure we provide the content our customers want to read.

If you would like to check out more books from Stormy Night Publications, if you want to learn more about our company, or if you would like to join our mailing list, please visit our website at:

www.stormynightpublications.com